T0367119
COMPLETE WORKS & OTHER STORIES
HOTEL
18 km
5km
60 km
20km
40km
PRESENTING

TEXAS
PAN AMERICAN
SERIES

COMPLETE WORKS & OTHER STORIES

AUGUSTO MONTERROSO

Translated by
Edith Grossman

with an introduction by
Will H. Corral

Copyright © 1995 by the University of Texas Press
All rights reserved
Printed in the United States of America

First edition, 1995
Published by arrangement with the author

Originally published as: *Obras completas (y otros cuentos)*, UNAM, México, 1959, and Ediciones Era, México, 1990. *Movimiento perpetuo*, Joaquín Mortiz, 1972, and Ediciones Era, México, 1991.

Requests for permission to reproduce material from this work should be sent to Permissions, University of Texas Press, P.O. Box 7819, Austin, TX 78713-7819.

⊗ The paper used in this publication meets the minimum requirements of American National Standard for Information Sciences—Permanence of Paper for Printed Library Materials, ANSI Z39.48-1984.

Library of Congress Cataloging-in-Publication Data

Monterroso, Augusto.
[Short stories. English]
Complete works and other stories / by Augusto Monterroso ; translated by Edith Grossman ; with an introduction by Will H. Corral.
p. cm. — (Texas Pan American series)
ISBN 0-292-75183-4 (cloth: alk. paper). — ISBN 0-292-75184-2 (pbk: alk. paper)
1. Monterroso, Augusto—Translations into English. I. Grossman, Edith, 1936– . II. Title. III. Series.
PQ7297.M62A613 1995
863—dc20 95-14550

Contents

PERPETUAL MOTION

For Bárbara Jacobs

Augusto Monterroso is one of the very few Latin American authors whose works are truly tailor-made for a comparative perspective on world literature. Rather than comparing Monterroso *to* other authors of the Western tradition, as seems to be the case for Latin American authors who are world renowned, one normally ends up perusing that tradition in terms *of* someone like Monterroso. Within the historical—but not aesthetic—relativity of such an assertion, the truth is that Monterroso is a precursor in many ways, serving as an enhancing presence for what is generally understood by "Latin American" literature. In the lecture series *Six Memos for the Next Millennium* (trans. Patrick Creagh, 1988), Italo Calvino discusses succinctly the universality and indispensability for literature of Lightness, Quickness, Exactitude, Visibility, and Multiplicity. Toward the end of the second lecture Calvino states:

> Borges and Bioy Casares put together an anthology of short extraordinary tales (*Cuentos breves y extraordinarios*, 1955). I would like to edit a collection of tales consisting of one sentence only, or even a single line. But so far I haven't found any to match the one by the Guatemalan writer Augusto Monterroso: "Cuando despertó, el dinosauro [sic] todavía estaba allí" (When I woke up, the dinosaur was still there). (51)[1]

Among those uncontestable (because they are neither static nor purely "Western") aesthetic values that Calvino does not discuss is the added element of greater ambiguity produced by Monterroso's original Spanish. By resorting to the perfectly grammatical deletion (surely on purpose) of the gendered Spanish pronoun "he" or "she" that could precede *despertó*, Monterroso enriches his text twofold. In this regard most if not all of the criticism about Monterroso and his work finds connections with the elements Calvino considers essential for literature. The linkages with other world authors from this century and before who have espoused parallel distillations about what good literature is and has always been will also become evident when reading the "stories" collected here.

Perhaps of equal importance in Calvino's admiration for Monterroso is the mention of Borges and Bioy Casares, whose 1955 collection serves to mark a "before" and "after." Much like his Argentine counterparts, Monterroso's notions of intertextuality, allusions, direct references, quotations, tributes, winks, and all the other anxieties of influence critics try to find in brilliant literature comprise an immediate and overwhelming legacy to Latin American literature. Yet his critics says "Monterroso is a postmodern minimalist" (along the lines of Heraclitus, Blake, Kierkegaard, Krauss, Cioran, or Canetti); "Monterroso is a humorist" (along the lines of Lem, Coover, D. Barthelme, or Groucho Marx); "Monterroso is a philosopher" (along the lines of Emerson, Nietzsche, or Wittgenstein's *zettel*). Yet he denies having anything to do with those models. As of this writing, such has been his *modus vivendi* for fifty years, and there is every hope among his huge Latin American following that there will be another Golden anniversary. The fact, however, is that for many years Monterroso was a "writer's writer." Now, despite his innermost wishes, he finds himself more deservedly canonical than any of the recently translated authors from the region.

At this juncture a generation of Latin American and Spanish readers and writers has read Monterroso, and his writing will continue to create precursors, happy emulators, and epigones. The rediscovery, critical institutionalization, and even popularization of his work in languages such as English are due to very evident reasons. Like the permanent lesson that can be culled from Borges in "Kafka and His Precursors," Monterroso allows his readers to say "Hey, [fill in the author] writes just like Monterroso." That is to say, the singularity of his literature brings him to the forefront. Nevertheless, he has never really cared about the commercialism that can propel an author to fame, perhaps because recognition among select intellectual minorities seems to be enough for him. However, as any theorist would argue, texts take on a life of their own once their authors hand in their manuscripts. Let us see, then, how we arrived at the present translation of his first two books.

What is the "before" and "after" to all this? Who is Augusto Monterroso? He has never really needed an introduction in Latin America, at least since José Donoso wrote the original Spanish version of *The Boom in Spanish American Literature: A Personal History* (trans. Gregory Kolovakos, 1977) a quarter of a century ago. Interestingly enough, other than a passing reference in interviews, the only time Monterroso has spoken about his personal life is in English, in some comments included in Angel Flores's *Spanish American Authors: The Twentieth Century* (1992). He states there that he comes from the Central American upper middle class, yet has had a life of economic hardship. Born in Honduras in 1921 to a Guatemalan father and Honduran mother, he is still a Guatemalan citizen. But what he seems to emphasize is the intellectual chronology of his learning:

> My studies were interrupted at an early age by my rejection of school and by my parents' continual travels between two different countries. Ever since I was a child, however, I have felt an inclination for the arts and especially for literature. I gave myself unknowingly to my love for them without thinking that one day I would be a writer. In other words, I am an autodidact; but I ought to add that what I learned in primary school and in a home full of literary and artistic currents had always pointed me in that direction (558).

He does add that while working at odd jobs and as an accounting assistant at a butcher shop he managed to study foreign languages (among his translations of books and essays are Swift's "A Modest Proposal") and to attend night classes at the Guatemalan National Library, where he "eagerly read the Spanish classics which are the foundation of my literary formation."

What Monterroso neglects to mention in typically modest fashion, although he refers to it in interviews, is his thorough knowledge, fondness for, and dialog with Greek and Roman classics (Catullus, Aesop, Juvenal, Vergil), Cervantes (for many years he taught a seminar on *Don Quixote* at the National University of Mexico), Góngora, Shakespeare, Johnson, Byron, Dante, Rilke, and, among his contemporaries, Borges. He is also quite reticent about his more contemporary influences, readings, and literary likes and dislikes. Monterroso is an outsider whose strength derives less from his experiments with those influences than from his vitality in producing from them an even more daring literary effect. But above all, his statement is not a euphemistic appraisal of his political commitment to progressive causes and the consequences he assumes as a result of his stance.[2] Wisely, instead of contributing to biographical fallacies, Monterroso lets his literature speak for if not about him. Suffice it to say that at this point his work has been translated into all the major languages of the world, including recent translations of the short stories collected here into Swedish, and of his fables into Latin and Chinese.

In this regard, it is time that we stop writing about how Monterroso and his work obsessively undermine the genres, laws, canons, and principles of major literature. Although he is famous for the type of concision and wit Calvino praises above, Monterroso's literature always was and will continue to be major. Clean and sharp, rarely harsh or lyrical, his prose is leavened with a dry, ever puckish and conceptual humor. Yet he has never conceded to being any kind of "humorist," nor has he fallen into the trap of admitting that serious things are said in jest. In the collections that follow the two included here, and in those that preceded them (two plaquettes from 1952 and 1953), we see the strict precision of a prose uncanny in its ability to suggest compassion for the human condition. It is a prose that offers vivid sights and personal insights, discordant sounds, and extremely rich sensations of body and mind. Monterroso's prose is supple, analytical, full of irony and intricate nuances. What also emerges in his work, especially in the dual collection presented here, is writing that peels away the social veneers that conceal the beast within human beings and reveals all that they have accomplished or undone throughout history.

Why, when such concerns and styles of writing are not "Latin American" but universal, has Monterroso been ensconced within the happy borders of his continent? The way in which Monterroso and his literary accomplices (among others, many Mexican poets) present their work and self-image to the public leaves no option other than to describe their narrative wisdom and common sense as "minor." In various moments and forums, many of us who have devoted a good part of our academic or everyday lives to Monterroso and his "complete works" have fallen into the trap of justifying his utter lack of conventionality as the rule of a minor literature. But the "stories" that follow confirm, after all, Monterroso's vitality as a major antidote to the verbal carelessness of an otherwise extremely rich Latin American literature. He is well aware of the misapprehensions that have accrued around his personal and writerly myths. But he also knows that his contradictions and the spareness of his publications are integral to those myths and to the public's appetite to see more of those oppositions in his writings.

This elegantly accurate translation by Edith Grossman contains the first two collections published by Monterroso. As a constant pursuer of *le mot juste* and *le bon mot* (at least once, when asked about how he wrote, he has answered "I don't write, I correct"), the time period between each of his works is long. Just when we think that we understand most of what Monterroso and his narrators are saying, and just when it seems that the only hope left is to see his work in an exquisite glossy journal, or as the sensible and serene critical intelligence included in a collection of scholarly criticism on the literature of the fantastic, or in a heartfelt tribute to Julio Cortázar, he comes up with another, entirely original work. When this happens there is always another critic who rediscovers Monterroso, or one to whom his previous work says something totally unheard of. This is the tension that a great writer always creates. It is a never-ending process, because besides these stories, Monterroso has published essays, criticism, apocryphal biographies, diaries, drawings, fragments, a prolog or two, translations, and all kinds of paratexts. If one adds to the above the Borgesean hybridity that informs many of his texts, the critic's task is equally endless.

Since his Mexican exile (generally permanent since 1944) Monterroso has been a pilgrim in many countries, the charming emissary of our subtle and shared Latin American specificities, and drawing from these, of the richness of the Spanish language. Rereading Edith Grossman's superb translation of Monterroso's very precise Spanish can finally convince one of the polemical notion that an original can also come alive in a version construed in another language, and that a translation can sometimes be a valid interpretation of a work which everyone says should not be translated.

Tangentially, the texts of these two collections also convince us, in yet another language, that it is possible for other readers to observe how much we Latin Americans owe to Monterroso. This is so mainly because, as the late Uruguayan critic Angel Rama wrote, Monterroso avoids "the rhetorical Latin American jungle." That is, even before the literary Boom of the sixties, modernity, albeit troubled, was part of our autochthonous patrimony. Moreover, Rama adds, Monterroso's technical sophistication and irreverence has put an end to the myth of Latin American literary tropicalism.

Rama rounds off his assertions with the comment that "Despite being a testimony of radical modernization, Monterroso's literature has not failed to secure a reelaboration of his regional culture, with which he has lucidly come to terms."

What we owe Monterroso is the consciousness of another way in which to define ourselves, or of what should define us. Thus, as many of the stories in *Complete Works (and Other Stories)* indicate, his writing is a way of decolonizing stereotypical representations and, more importantly, avoiding the critical postcolonization of our literature by the specter of those who tell us what should be politically correct for a Latin American. It is no coincidence that when the Latin American writers of the last two decades assume testimonial responsibility (fraught with personal danger) in history, Monterroso and his work are an obligatory point of origin in which to find the bases of commitment.

The above is generally perceived by critics who write *from* Latin America. (I refer to mental states, not locations of culture.) We have always known that the subaltern can speak (ongoing indigenous struggles attest eloquently to that), and this is why, when confronted by the new imperial I's of the English-only "first world" (see "Mister Taylor" and "First Lady"), Monterroso's characters almost invariably win, and even choose to be modern. For better or worse, the hardly essentialist practice of letting Latin Americans decide for themselves fits into a current problem of the nineties. This is the issue of who or what is deciding the canon of texts that make up the literature of our America that should be taught or heeded. Because of such conflicts, when one reads a fantastically ingenious writer like Monterroso the unavoidable question is whether he is merely witty. The immediate answer is no, because he is both serious and daring in his approach to style. Thus, his critics have had a hard time grasping the originality of his social commentary. Monterroso fascinates and confuses us, he shakes us out of our complacency and neat little mental boxes. Monterroso ultimately cures us of the mistaken belief that we can write about an author about whom our perceptions cannot change.

In the end, like the title essay-story in *Perpetual Motion*, he becomes a fly we can never catch. Nevertheless, and to his great embarrassment, Monterroso is now well known, quoted and published. Today, without promotional campaigns or introductions like this one, his declarations, novel ideas, and idiosyncracies easily become popular news or the quote of the day. So when he wants to let his critics rest, Monterroso writes aphorisms, dedications, vignettes, newspaper articles, epitaphs, and the like. As a result of these acts of integration and assimilation, his interpreters can only begin to decipher his perpetual literature, and we always return to the exceptional paradox that any new work by Monterroso can be. His literature, like his life, is an experience of limits, and these are ours. In his prose, the interpreter's or the interpreted's positions can sustain the fiction that the person who writes and the person about whom one writes are a single seamless entity. By extension, his texts also correct the fallacy of believing that a primary characteristic of "minor" literature is that everything in it is either aesthetic or political. Orwell, who believed it impossible to avoid politics in our century, reminds us that politics can also be a bunch of lies, evasions, madness, hate, and schizophrenia. Perhaps because of this, and due to the imminent danger of decontextualizing, it is better to realize that we sometimes propose readings that contradict our convictions.

The "after" in Monterroso is never a full departure from his beginning, because his texts make manifest a consciousness that after centuries of shared human experiences almost everything has been thought of and written about. This perception of the creative process does not refer to his own works, because they are not variations on a theme. Between the two collections you are about to read he published *La oveja negra y demás fábulas* [The Black Sheep and other Fables], whose polyvalence totally renovates the notion that such texts (fables) place their readers in front of a mirror. After these three collections he abandons the pithiness of their form for *Lo demás es silencio (La vida y la obra de Eduardo Torres)* [The Rest is Silence (The Life and Works of Eduardo Torres) (1978)], an apocryphal biography of a small town intellectual. Presented in four parts as the testimony of friends, family, and wife; as an anthology of the farcical and honest Torres; and as a collection of his aphorisms, sayings, and "literary criticism," the text caused hilarious reactions among Mexico City *literati*, ready to cry foul and accuse the "fictitious" and "real" author of libel and other non-literary offenses. In 1987 the "after" meanders toward the diary form with *La letra e (fragmentos de un diario)* [The Letter e (Fragments of a Diary)]. Again, "diary" is a convenient generic label, because the author always seems ready to let his new readers slide easily into his world and then shock them with the strategies, codes, and narrative economies that define him.

His most recent work to date is *Los buscadores de oro* [The Gold Searchers (1993)], which as autobiography contains a lyricism and imagery that, of course, only serve to present new possibilities for the genre. Once again, if what Monterroso employs as thematics is seen as clairvoyant, there is the added element of timeliness. In the first half of this last decade of the century Vargas Llosa, Bryce Echenique, Bioy Casares, Arenas, Paz, the late Ribeyro, and Arreola (told to Fernando del Paso) have felt compelled to write partial or complete autobiographies. However, as the master of brevity, in the sense of a Gracián, Monterroso outdoes them all by writing the shortest one, devoted to the shortest life period, in the briefest chronological sense. Between and among these works there have been critical editions, translations, a plethora of literary awards and national and international honors, anthologies of his works, at least five *festschriften*, a film about his life, a stint as the Edward Laroque Tinker Visiting Professor at Stanford, memberships in editorial boards, and his appointment to the Academia Guatemalteca de la Lengua. It is within the context of all the preceding events that the collections included here can be understood, and reading them will prove the futility of discussing their contents in full. Nevertheless, let us go to the "before" Monterroso with at least an inkling of what he does there, because there is no grand gesture as art in that period.

Complete Works (and Other Stories) has acquired a wide public beyond the confines of the elite Spanish American literary circles that found in its stories, always surprising in form and content, scathing allusions to the weaknesses and defects of the artistic or intellectual world. Once again, and now in English, we see clearly that behind all brilliant satire lies a sense of compassion, that this work's scope is expansive, and that its nimble variety reaches us all. Those who search for symbols in this book do well. But those who do not will no doubt find them, as long as they are not afraid to confront their own images at every turn of the page. Here Monterroso shows the knack of creating ordinary and unusual characters (Mister Taylor, Fombona, the First Lady) bruised by the meaninglessness of their existence. Yet their ingratiating simplicity merges with the author's unswerving faith in humanity's ability to represent itself. Other stories, whose allusions to Western imperialism are clear, prove to us that the struggle over historical and social meaning is part of human history. This collection presents Monterroso at his full range, from ironically sublime to abruptly colloquial. There are endless elliptical asides, recondite images, thematic innovations, metatextual games, and exploits with time and space, all heightened by the energy with which his language is embued.

If the long interval between his books has been a source of frustration for readers, the reality is that to this day he has not repeated himself. As its name indicates, *Perpetual Motion* is a book whose pages dread the horror of stability. Visually, for example, the random placement of epigraphs (not always related to the texts that precede or follow them) is a means of fashioning the book as object. To the exasperation of linear spirits, these pages pass from theme to theme and from one genre to another with the courage that only the fear of repetition or closure provides. Perhaps this work's greatest virtue (according to its author) is that it can be acquired or not, retained or not, without anything happening to the readers, the author, or the universe. Here, then, is one of the few decidedly dispensable books of all time—a rare quality today and always. For this reason there will be eager readers (hence it is being published) who will consider this book essential, if only to reaffirm their faith in gratuitous acts. This is the case with the very moving story "The Maids," where the sheer succulence of the author's language leaps from the page, leaving us to ponder its social criticism. Language is no less the protagonist in "essays" such as "Flies" and "You Tell Sarabia . . ." In these hybrid texts reality is mediated through montage. Yet there is the sense that we know perfectly all that the narrators are trying to tell us.

So what or who comes "after" Monterroso? If we were to answer based on what he accomplishes in these two collections, we would come up with a list of untranslated Spanish American authors as well as with the names of some canonical authors. They are the non-so-new breed of what Rubén Darío once called "the odd ones," and, like Monterroso, their rebellious attitudes against stilted forms and received ideas regarding literariness has characterized every moment of their lives. After all, it is Monterroso who invents the new genre called "perpetual motion," and later on, in his 1983 collection *La palabra mágica* [The Magic Word], posits and expounds on the obituary as a new genre. Thus the names of Spanish American authors like Felisberto Hernández, José Antonio Ramos Sucre, Roberto Arlt, Macedonio Fernández, Pablo Palacio, Julio Garmendia, Julio Torri, and Antonio Porchia come to mind for the first half of this century. Juan José Arreola, Oliverio Girondo, Virgilio Piñera, Julio Ramón Ribeyro, Julio Cortázar, and Jorge Luis Borges immediately come to mind for the period of the Boom. More recently, there are Mario Benedetti, Salvador Elizondo, Eduardo Galeano, Pía Barros, and many others. Like them, Monterroso explains that merely for the sake of "going native" critics and common readers alike should never suppress the cultural, ideological, and institutional contexts within which such authors write.

Latin American prose at the end of the twentieth century is an elegant bookstore and library, constructed like a solipsistic Escher painting, or, even more recently, like Mark Tansey's wry explorations or artistic issues through imaginary narratives whose background texture is made up of letters. To go from one of the library's or bookstore's shelves to another, its readers have to pass through deconstructionist literary minefields, through a central hall with no symmetry, or through chains of solutions decorated with the metaphors of the books we have read. Everyone has to pass through the central hall (the reference room as it were) that connects all the rooms in that library, but no one outside of it knows that a central hall exists. From now on let us call that central hall the almost complete works of Augusto Monterroso. Its doors open in every direction, to all the missing links we have been searching for, and with all the scepticism, ire, passion, and amusement we need. His work is, in the final analysis, a testimony to a love of literature and the condition of Latin American culture. His positive displacement of genre constraints does not mean ideological abandonment, nor a reliance on the schlock and schmaltz of popularizers. Rather, his commitment is to the ethics of a writer and his writing, with the most pristine expression of the components of a life devoted to literature.

WILL H. CORRAL

1. *Six Memos for the Next Millennium* is a translation from the Italian manuscript of five of six lectures planned by Calvino before his death in September, 1985. Calvino did not finish the sixth lecture, which, according to his wife, would have been on Consistency.

2. Monterroso has published the first volume of his autobiography, *Los buscadores de oro* [The Gold Searchers (1993)], now distributed in the United States in the original Spanish by Vintage. This installment covers the years of his childhood up to 1936. The only previous book of Monterroso's published in English is a translation of his 1969 fable collection *The Black Sheep and Other Fables* (trans. Walter I. Bradbury, 1971). A selection of academic and general criticism on his narrative and nonfiction prose, plus primary and secondary bibliographies that include interviews, is being published under the title *Augusto Monterroso ante la crítica*, ed. Will H. Corral (Mexico City: UNAM/Era, 1995). Please refer to this collection for complete entries for the items mentioned in this introduction.

COMPLETE WORKS (AND OTHER STORIES)

MISTER TAYLOR

"Somewhat less strange, though surely more exemplary," the other man said, "is the story of Mr. Percy Taylor, a headhunter in the Amazon jungle.

In 1937 he is known to have left Boston, Massachusetts, where he so refined his spirit that he did not have a penny to his name. In 1944 he appears for the first time in South America, in the Amazon region, living with the Indians of a tribe whose name there is no need to recall.

Because of the shadows under his eyes and his famished appearance, he soon became known as 'The Gringo Beggar,' and even the schoolchildren pointed at him and threw stones when he passed by, his beard gleaming in the golden tropical sun. But this caused no distress to Mr. Taylor's humble nature, for he had read in the first volume of William C. Knight's *Complete Works* that poverty is no disgrace if one does not envy the rich.

In a few weeks the natives grew accustomed to him and his

outlandish clothing. Furthermore, since he had blue eyes and a vaguely foreign accent, the President and the Minister of Foreign Affairs were fearful of provoking an international incident and treated him with singular respect.

He was so wretchedly poor that one day he went into the jungle to search for edible plants. He had walked several yards, not daring to turn his head, when by sheerest accident he happened to see a pair of Indian eyes observing him carefully from the underbrush. A long shudder traveled down Mr. Taylor's sensitive spine. But the intrepid Mr. Taylor defied all danger and continued on his way, whistling as if he had seen nothing.

With a leap (why call it feline?) the native landed in front of him and cried:

'Buy head? Money money.'

Although his English could not have been worse, Mr. Taylor, feeling somewhat ill, realized that the Indian was offering to sell him the oddly shrunken human head he carried in his hand.

Mr. Taylor, of course, was in no position to buy it, but since he appeared not to understand what had been said, the Indian was horribly embarrassed at not speaking good English and, begging his pardon, gave it to him as a gift.

Mr. Taylor felt great joy as he returned to his hut. That night, lying on his back on the precarious palm mat that was his bed, and interrupted only by the buzz of passionate flies that circled round him as they made obscene love, Mr. Taylor spent a long while contemplating his curious acquisition with delight. He derived the greatest aesthetic pleasure from counting the hairs of the beard and mustache, one by one, and looking straight into the rather ironic eyes that seemed to smile at him in gratitude for his attention.

A man of enormous culture, Mr. Taylor was accustomed to contemplation, but this time he soon wearied of his philosophical reflections and decided to present the head to his uncle, Mr. Rolston, who lived in New York and who, from his earliest childhood, had shown a lively interest in the cultural manifestations of the Spanish-American peoples.

A few days later, Mr. Taylor's uncle asked him (even before inquiring after the important state of his health) to please favor him with five more. Mr. Taylor willingly satisfied Mr. Rolston's desire—no one knows how—by return mail, saying he was 'very happy to fulfill the request.' An extremely grateful Mr. Rolston asked for another ten. Mr. Taylor was 'delighted to be of service.' But the following month, when he was asked to send twenty more, Mr. Taylor, simple and bearded but with a refined artistic sensibility, suspected that his mother's brother was selling them at a profit.

And, to tell the truth, he was. With complete honesty Mr. Rolston informed him of the fact in an inspired letter whose strictly businesslike terms made the strings of Mr. Taylor's sensitive spirit vibrate as never before.

They immediately formed a corporation, Mr. Taylor agreeing to obtain and ship large quantities of shrunken heads that Mr. Rolston would sell in his country at the highest possible price.

At first there were some bothersome difficulties with certain local residents. But Mr. Taylor, who in Boston had received the highest grades for his essay on Joseph Henry Silliman, proved to be a skilled politician and obtained from the authorities not only the necessary export license but an exclusive ninety-nine-year concession as well. It was not difficult to convince the Chief Executive Warrior and the Legislative Medicine Men that this patriotic move would enrich the community, and that soon all the thirsty aborigines (whenever they paused to refresh themselves while collecting heads) could have an ice-cold soft drink whose magic formula he himself would supply.

When the members of the Cabinet, after a brief but brilliant exercise of intellect, became aware of these advantages, their love of country welled up and in three days they issued a decree ordering the people to speed up their production of shrunken heads.

Some months later, in Mr. Taylor's country, the heads had gained the popularity we all remember. At first they were the privilege of the wealthiest families, but democracy is democracy, and no one will deny that in a matter of weeks even schoolteachers could buy them.

A home without its shrunken head was deemed a home that had

failed. Soon the collectors appeared, bringing with them certain contradictions: owning seventeen heads was considered bad taste, but having eleven was distinguished. Heads became so popular that the really elegant people began to lose interest and would acquire one only if it possessed some peculiarity that saved it from the commonplace. A very rare head with Prussian whiskers, which in life had belonged to a highly decorated general, was presented to the Danfeller Institute, which in turn made an immediate grant of three and a half million dollars to further the development of this exciting cultural manifestation of the peoples of Latin America.

In the meantime, the tribe had made so much progress it now had its own path around the Legislative Palace. On Sundays and on Independence Day, the members of Congress would ride the bicycles they had received from the Company along that merry path, clearing their throats, displaying their feathers, and laughing very seriously.

But it was inevitable. Not all times are good times. The first shortage of heads occurred without warning.

Then the best part of the fiesta began.

Natural deaths no longer sufficed. The Minister of Public Health considered himself a sincere man, and one dark night when the lights were out he caressed his wife's breast as if he would never stop and confessed to her that he thought he was incapable of raising mortality rates to a level that would satisfy the interests of the Company, to which she replied that he should not worry, that he would see how everything would turn out all right and the best thing now would be for them to go to sleep.

Strong measures were necessary to compensate for this administrative deficiency, and a harsh death penalty was imposed.

The jurists consulted with one another and raised even the smallest shortcoming to the category of a crime punishable by hanging or the firing squad, depending on the seriousness of the infraction.

Even simple mistakes became criminal acts. For example, if in the course of an ordinary conversation someone said carelessly 'It's very hot,' and later it could be proven, thermometer in hand, that it really was not hot at all, that person was charged a small fine and immediately executed, his head sent on to the Company and, it must be said in all fairness, his trunk and limbs returned to the bereaved.

The legislation dealing with disease had wide repercussions and was frequently discussed by the Diplomatic Corps and in the embassies of friendly powers.

According to this remarkable law, the gravely ill were given twenty-four hours to put their affairs in order and die, but if in this time they had the good fortune to infect their families, they received a month-long reprieve for each relative they infected. Victims of minor illnesses, and those who simply did not feel well, deserved the scorn of the entire nation, and any passerby was entitled to spit in their faces. For the first time in history the importance of doctors who cured no one was recognized (there were several candidates for the Nobel prize among them). Dying became an example of the highest patriotism, not only on the national level but on an even more glorious continental scale.

With the growth achieved by subsidiary industries (coffin manufacturing, for example, flourished with the technical assistance of the Company), the country entered a period of what is called great economic prosperity. This progress was particularly evident in a new flowered path on which the deputies' wives would stroll, their pretty little heads enveloped in the melancholy of golden autumnal afternoons as they nodded yes, yes, everything was fine, in response to the inquiries of some journalist on the other path who greeted them with a smile and tipped his hat.

I remember in passing that one of these journalists, who on a certain occasion emitted a thunderstorm of a sneeze that he could not explain, was accused of extremism and put against the wall of the firing squad. Only after his unselfish end did the academicians of the language recognize that the journalist had one of the fattest heads in the country, but when it was shrunk it turned out so well that no one could tell the difference.

And Mr. Taylor? By this time he had been named Special Adviser to the Constitutional President. As an example of what private initiative can accomplish, he now counted his thousands by the thousands, but he lost no sleep over this for he had read in the final volume of William C. Knight's *Complete Works* that being a millionaire is no disgrace if one does not despise the poor.

As I believe I have already mentioned, not all times are good times.

Given the prosperity of the enterprise, the moment arrived when the only people left were the authorities and their wives, and the journalists and their wives. Without too much effort Mr. Taylor concluded that the only possible solution was to declare war on the neighboring tribes. Why not? This was progress.

With the help of a few small cannon, the first tribe was neatly beheaded in just under three months. Mr. Taylor tasted the glory of expanding his domain. Then came the second tribe, then the third, the fourth, and the fifth. Progress spread so rapidly that soon, regardless of the efforts of the technicians, they could find no neighboring tribes to make war on.

It was the beginning of the end.

The little paths began to languish. Only occasionally did one see a lady or some poet laureate with a book under his arm taking a stroll. The weeds again overran the two paths, making the way difficult and thorny for the delicate feet of the ladies. Along with the heads, the number of bicycles had thinned out, and the joyful, optimistic greetings had almost disappeared.

The coffin manufacturer was gloomier and more funereal than ever. And everyone felt as if they had just remembered a pleasant dream, one of those wonderful dreams when you find a purse full of gold coins and put it under your pillow and go back to sleep and very early the next day, when you awake, you look for it and find nothing but emptiness.

Business, unfortunately, went on as usual, but people had trouble sleeping, fearful they would wake up exported.

In Mr. Taylor's country, of course, the demand continued to grow. New substitutes appeared daily but fooled no one, and people insisted on the little heads from Latin America.

The final crisis was near. A desperate Mr. Rolston constantly demanded more heads. Although the Company's stocks suffered a sharp decline, Mr. Rolston was certain his nephew would do something to save the situation.

Daily shipments decreased to one a month, and even then they included anything: children's heads, ladies' heads, even deputies' heads.

Suddenly it was all over.

One harsh, gray Friday, home from the Stock Exchange and still dazed by the shouting of his friends and their lamentable display of panic, Mr. Rolston resolved to jump out the window (rather than use a gun—the noise would have terrified him) after he opened a package that had come in the mail and found the shrunken head of Mr. Taylor smiling at him from a distance, from the wild Amazon, with a false boyish smile that seemed to say 'I'm sorry, I'm really sorry, I won't do it again.'"

ONE OUT OF THREE

> I prefer to find someone who would rather listen to my stories than tell me his.
>
> PLAUTUS

I have already estimated your surprise at receiving this letter. It is also likely that at first you will take it as a cruel joke, and almost certain that your first impulse will be to destroy it, to throw it as far away as you can. And yet, if you do, you could hardly commit a more serious error. Let it be said in your defense that you would not be the first to make that mistake, or the last to regret it, of course.

I will tell you in all honesty that I feel sorry for you. But my feeling is not only natural—it also conforms to your own desires. You belong to that gloomy segment of humanity who finds relief for your sorrow in the pity of others. I beg you to take heart: There is nothing unusual about your case. One out of three people looks for nothing else, although they do so in the most devious ways. The person who complains of a disease as severe as it is imaginary, the woman who declares herself overwhelmed by the heavy burden of her domestic duties, the man who publishes plaintive verse (regardless of whether it is good or bad)—all of them are pleading, in the interest of all the others, for a little of the compassion they dare not offer themselves. You are more honorable: You scorn the versification of your bitterness, with elegant decorum you hide the outpouring of energy your daily bread demands, you do not pretend to be ill. You simply tell your story, and, as if you were doing your friends a kind favor, you ask their advice with the secret intention of not following it.

You must be curious as to how I learned of your problem. Nothing could be simpler: It is my profession. In due course I will reveal to you what that profession is.

To continue: Three days ago, under an uncommon morning sun, you boarded a bus at the corner of Reforma and Sevilla. The people waiting for these vehicles frequently wear a disconcerted expression of surprise if they glimpse a familiar face in the crowd. How different you were! All I needed to see was the gleam in your eye when you caught sight of a face you recognized among the perspiring passengers, and I was certain I had found one of my clients.

Following a professional custom, I eavesdropped on your conversation. In fact, as soon as you had dispensed as quickly as possible with the obligatory greetings, you began the inevitable recounting of your misfortunes. There was no longer any doubt in my mind. Your narration of events made it easy to see that your friend had received the same confidences no more than twenty-four hours earlier. Following you for the rest of the day until I learned where you lived was, as usual, the part of my duties I enjoyed the most, although the reason for this escapes me.

I don't know if it will anger or please you, but I must repeat that your case is not unique. I will explain briefly the history of your current situation. And if I am wrong—though I doubt it—the mistake will merely be the exception that proves the ineluctable rule.

You are suffering from one of the most common afflictions of the human race: the need to communicate with your fellow man. Since attaining the power of speech, man has found nothing as agreeable as a friend who will listen with interest as he talks about his sorrows and joys. Not even love can equal this feeling. There are those who are content with one friend. For others, a thousand are not enough. You belong to the latter group, and this simple fact is the origin of your sorrow and my profession.

I would go so far as to swear that it all began when you told an intimate friend of your difficulties in love, and he listened attentively until you had finished, and offered you the best advice he could. But you—and here is where the endless chain begins—you did not think his prescriptions were sound. If he insisted that you go to the root of the problem, as they say, and end it, you found more than one reason for not giving up the struggle. If he advised continuing the siege until you had conquered the fortress, you were drowned in pessimism and saw everything as dark and hopeless. It is only a small step from this to looking for the remedy in another person. How many steps did you take?

You began a hopeful pilgrimage through your crowded address book. You even attempted (with increasing success) to make new friends with whom you could begin to discuss your problem. It is no surprise: Suddenly you noticed that the day has only twenty-four hours, and that this astronomical lack of consideration was an enormous factor working against you. You had to expand your means of travel and plan your schedule with fine precision. The methodical use of the telephone helped, and it certainly broadened your possibilities, but this antiquated system is still a luxury, and sixty percent of those whom you want to keep informed do not have this dubious advantage in their homes.

Not content with late nights and too little sleep, you began to get up at dawn to grasp at a time that passed more and more quickly and was irreparably lost. The neglect of your appearance was flagrant: Your beard was unkempt, your once impeccable trousers sagged at the knees, and a hard gray dust covered your shoes like an affliction. It seemed unfair, but you had to accept the fact that even if you awoke at dawn full of enthusiasm, you had no friends willing to share your morning passion. And so—obviously—the inevitable moment has arrived: You have become physically incapable of keeping your wide circle of acquaintances up-to-date.

That moment is also my moment. For a modest monthly fee, I can offer you the perfect solution. If you accept—and I can assure you that you will because you have no other choice—you can forget forever your incessant traveling, your baggy trousers, the dust, your beard, the tedious phone messages.

In short, I am prepared to offer you a first-rate specialized radio broadcast. Due to the regrettable passing of a former client seriously affected by the program of Land Reform, at present I have at my disposal a quarter of an hour; considering how far your confidences have gone, this would be more than ample to keep your friends informed—not only to the day but to the minute—regarding your truly extraordinary case.

It would probably be *de trop* to enumerate in detail the advantages of my system, but I would like to outline some of them for you.

1. A soothing effect on your nervous system is guaranteed from the first day.

2. Discretion is guaranteed. Although your voice will be heard by any individual who owns a radio, I consider it highly unlikely that persons not your friends would wish to continue a confidence whose background they do not know. In this way, we can reject any possibility of morbid curiosity.

3. Many of your friends (who now listen unwillingly to the personal version) would take an active interest in the broadcast if you merely mentioned their names, either openly or indirectly.

4. All of your acquaintances would be informed at the same time of the same facts, thereby avoiding jealousy and subsequent recriminations, since only their carelessness, or a chance malfunction of their radios, would place them at a disadvantage with re-

spect to any of the others. To eliminate this depressing possibility, each broadcast begins with a brief synopsis of what was narrated previously.

5. Whenever you think it appropriate, the story can be made more interesting and varied, and more entertaining, with illustrative excerpts from operatic arias (I will not insist on the sentimental richness of Italian opera) and selections from the great masters. The proper musical background is an absolute necessity, and an extensive record collection containing the most astonishing sounds produced by man or nature is at the disposal of every subscriber.

6. The narrator does not see his listener's face, thus bypassing all kinds of inhibitions for him as well as for those who hear him.

7. Since the program is aired once a day for fifteen minutes, the confidential narrator has an additional twenty-three hours and forty-five minutes to prepare his text and definitively avoid annoying contradictions and involuntary lapses of memory.

8. If your story is successful and a significant number of spontaneous listeners join your friends and acquaintances, it will not be difficult to find a sponsor, thus adding to the benefits I have already indicated a solid financial profit which, as it grows, would open the possibility of absorbing the entire twenty-four-hour day and turning a simple fifteen-minute broadcast into an ongoing, uninterrupted program. To be perfectly frank, this has not yet occurred, but it could with a man of your talent.

Mine is a message of hope. Have faith. For now, concentrate on this: The world is full of people like you. Tune your radio to 1373 kilocycles on the 720-meter band. At any hour of the day or night, winter or summer, rain or shine, you will hear the most diverse, surprising voices filled with a melancholy serenity: a captain who for the past fourteen years has been telling how his ship went down in a blind storm but he did not make the decision to share its fate; a careful woman who lost her only son during the riot-filled night of September 15; a traitor tormented by remorse; a former dictator of a Central American republic; a ventriloquist. All endlessly telling their stories. All asking for compassion.

FINISHED SYMPHONY

"And I could tell you," the fat man interjected in a rush, "that three years ago in Guatemala an old organist in a neighborhood church told me that in 1929 when he was asked to catalogue the music manuscripts in La Merced he suddenly found some unusual pages that intrigued him and he began to study them with his usual devotion and because the notes in the margins were written in German it took him a long time to realize they were the two final movements of the *Unfinished Symphony* so I could just imagine his feelings when he saw Schubert's signature written clearly and when he ran out to the street in great excitement to tell everyone of his discovery they laughed and said he had lost his mind and wanted to trick them but since he was a master of his craft and knew with certainty that the last two movements were as excellent as the first two he did not lose heart but swore instead to devote the rest of his life to making people admit the validity of his discovery and that was why from then on he dedicated himself to methodically visiting every musician in Guatemala with such awful results that after fighting with most of them and without saying anything to anybody least of all his wife he sold his house and went to Europe and once he was in Vienna it was even worse because they said no Guatemalan *Leiermann** was going to teach them how to find lost works least of all ones by Schubert whose scholars were all over the city and how could those pages have ended up so far from home until almost desperate and with only enough money for his return passage he met a family of elderly Jews who had lived in Buenos Aires and spoke Spanish and listened to him very attentively and became very agitated when God knows how they played the two movements on their piano viola and violin and at last grew tired of examining the pages every which way and smelling them and holding them up to the light that came in through the window and finally found themselves obliged to admit at first very quietly and then with great shouts they're by Schubert! they're by Schubert! and began to cry in despair on each other's shoulders as if instead of finding the pages they had just lost them and I would have been amazed at how they continued to cry although they calmed down a little and after talking among themselves in their own language tried to convince him as they rubbed their hands together that the movements excellent as they were added nothing to the value of the symphony just as it was and on the contrary one could say they detracted from it since people had grown used to the legend that Schubert tore them up or did not even try to write them certain he would never surpass or even equal the quality of the first two and the pleasure lay in thinking if this is how the *allegro* and the *andante* are what must the *scherzo* and the *allegro ma non troppo* be like and if he really respected and revered the memory of Schubert the most intelligent thing would be to allow them to keep the music because besides the fact that there would be an endless polemic the only one who would lose anything would be Schubert and then convinced he could never achieve anything among the philistines much less the admirers of Schubert who were even worse he sailed back to Guatemala and one night during the crossing under a full moon shining against the foaming sides

*organ-grinder

of the ship with the deepest sadness and sick of fighting bad people and good he took the manuscript and ripped the pages one by one and threw the pieces overboard until he was certain that now no one would ever find them again"—the fat man concluded in a certain tone of affected melancholy—"while great tears burned his cheeks and he thought bitterly that neither he nor his country would ever claim the glory of having returned to the world those pages that the world should have received with so much joy but which the world with so much common sense had rejected."

FIRST LADY

"My husband says it's just another one of my dumb ideas," she thought, "but all he wants is for me to stay home all the time, slaving like I used to. And that's just what he won't get. Maybe the others are afraid of him but not me. If I hadn't helped him when we were really broke, we'd still be in a mess. And why shouldn't I recite poetry if I want to, if I like it? He's President now but that shouldn't stand in my way—he should realize that this way I can help him even more. The fact is that men, presidents or not, are full of their own dumb ideas. Besides, I wouldn't run around giving recitals any old place like a lunatic, just at official functions or benefits. Yes sir, there's nothing wrong with that."

There was nothing wrong with it. She finished her bath. She went into her bedroom. While she was combing her hair, she saw in the mirror the shelves behind her. They were filled with books in disarray. Novels. Poetry. She thought about some of them and how much she liked them. Anthologies of the thousand best poems in the world, no one had surpassed those giants and reciters of poetry—she had marked the most beautiful ones with little strips of paper. "Laughing with Tears in My Eyes," "The Rabbi's Head," "Tropics!" "To a Mother." My God, where did they find so many things to write about? Soon there'd be no more room for books in the house. But even if you couldn't read them all, they were the best legacy.

Several copies of that night's program were on the dresser. She really felt like giving a reading all by herself. Until now, because she was so modest, she had not arranged anything like that. She knew, though, that she was the principal performer.

This time it was a benefit that had been organized in something of a hurry for the School Breakfast Program. Someone had noticed that schoolchildren were undernourished and that some of them were fainting at about eleven in the morning, probably the very moment when the teachers were at their best. At first it was attributed to indigestion, then to an epidemic of worms (Department of Health), and only recently, during one of his frequent attacks of insomnia, did it occur in a hazy way to the Director General of Education that they might possibly be cases of hunger.

When the Director General called a good number of parents to a meeting, most of them objected loudly to the idea that they might be so poor, and for the sake of their pride, none was inclined to believe what he said. But when the meeting adjourned, several approached the Director individually and confessed that sometimes—not always of course—they sent their children to school on an empty stomach. The Director was horrified at seeing his suspicions confirmed and decided it was necessary to do something soon. Fortunately, he remembered that the President had been his classmate in high school, and he arranged to see him immediately. He did not regret it. The President received him in the nicest way, probably with more cordiality than he would have displayed had he occupied a less elevated position. So that when he began, "Mr. President . . ." he laughed and said, "Cut out the 'Mr. President' crap and tell me straight out why you're here," and laughing all the while he made him sit down with a light pressure on his shoulder. Things were going fine. But the Director knew that no matter how many slaps on the back he gave him, things were not the way they were back in the days when they were in school together, or even two years ago when they would have a drink with friends at the Danubio. In any event, he was obviously beginning to feel comfortable in his office. As he himself had said as he raised his index finger over dessert at a recent dinner at his parents' house, first to the general anticipation and then to the thunderous applause of his relatives and comrades-in-arms: "At first it feels strange, but you get used to everything."

"Well sir, what brings you here?" he insisted. "I'll bet you're already having problems at the Ministry."

"Well, to tell the truth, I am."

"Izzat so?" said the President triumphantly, approving his own cleverness.

"But, if you'll permit me, that's not why I've come. I'll tell you about that another time. Look, I won't waste your time, I'll be completely frank. The thing is, there have been several cases of children fainting with hunger at school, and I'd like to see what we can do about it. I prefer telling you directly because if I don't it means just running from one office to the other. Besides, it's better for me to be the one to tell you because there's bound to be somebody else who'll say I'm not doing my job. My idea is for you to authorize me to try to get some money and set up a kind of semi-official Milk Fund."

"You're not turning communist on me, are you?" he interrupted, laughing out loud. Here is where you could see the wonderful mood he was in that day. They both laughed a good deal. The Director joked and warned him to watch out because he was reading a little book on Marxism, to which he replied, still laughing, that he better not go to see the Director of Police because he might really get fucked over. After exchanging more witticisms on the same subject, he said it seemed like a good idea to him, that he should see who he could get money from, that he should say he agreed, and maybe UNICEF could give them a little more milk. "The gringos have milk up the ass," he declared finally, standing and ending the interview.

"Oh, and listen," he added when the Director was already halfway out the door, "maybe you want to talk to my wife about helping you. She likes that kind of thing."

The Director told him fine and that he would speak to her right away.

It really depressed him, though, because he didn't like working with women—least of all officials' wives. Most of them were strange, vain, difficult, and you always had to worry about being polite enough, making sure they were always sitting down, and becoming nervous if for some reason you had to tell them no. Besides, he didn't know her very well. But the smartest thing would be to take the President's suggestion as an order.

When he spoke to her, she accepted immediately. Could there be any doubt? She would not only help by talking to her friends, but she would personally work enthusiastically and take part, for example, in any benefits that would be organized.

"I can recite poetry," she said; "you know I've always done it as an amateur." "How nice," she thought as she talked to him, "that I have this chance." But at the same time she regretted the thought and was afraid God would punish her when she reflected on the fact that it wasn't nice for children to faint with hunger. "Poor things," she thought quickly to placate heaven and avoid punishment. And aloud she said:

"Poor babies. And they keep on fainting?"

The Director explained patiently that the same ones did not keep fainting regularly, but sometimes it was one, sometimes another, and the best thing was to try to give breakfast to the greatest number possible. They would have to set up an organization for collecting money.

"Of course," she said. "What will we call it?"

"What do you think of 'School Breakfast Program'?" said the Director.

She ran her hand over the program, an elegantly printed rectangle of satinized paper:

1. Introductory Remarks by the Honorable Hugo Miranda, Director General of Education of the Ministry of Public Education.

2. Barcarolle from the "Tales of Hoffman," by Offenbach, performed by students from the Fourth of July School.

3. Three Waltzes by Chopin, performed by René Elgueta, student at the National Conservatory.

4. "The Motives of the Wolf," by Rubén Darío, performed by Her Excellency Doña Eulalia Fernández de Rivera González, First Lady of the Republic.

5. "My Fatherland's Skies," by the National Composer Don Federico Díaz, with the composer at the piano.

6. National Anthem.

She thought it looked fine. Although maybe there was too much music and not enough reciting.

"Do you like what I'm going to recite?" she asked her husband.

"As long as you don't forget it halfway through and make a fool of yourself," he answered, annoyed but incapable of seriously opposing her. "I swear I don't know why you got involved in this dumb business. As if you didn't know how stupid the boys are. Before you know it they'll be making jokes about you. But when you get an idea in your head there's no talking to you."

Back when he was in love with her he had wanted her to recite and even asked her to do it so she'd like him more. But now it was a different story, and her public appearances irritated him.

"Atwhay Iyaay asay isay uetray, ightray?" she thought. "They can't stand for his wife to have any initiative because then right away they start objecting and just want to complicate everything."

"How could I forget it?" she said aloud, getting up to look for a handkerchief. "I've known it since I was a kid. What I don't like is having this little cold. But I think maybe it's nerves. Every time I have to do something important on a certain date I'm afraid I'll get sick and I start thinking: Now I'm going to catch cold, now I'm going to catch cold, until I really have one. Yes sir. It must be nerves. The proof is I'm always better afterwards."

Suddenly she saw herself in the mirror, raised her arms, and tried out her voice:

The maaan with the heaaart of a leely
sooul of a cheerub, celeeestial tooungue
the humble and sweeeet
Fraaancis of Asiiisi
zwith
  a roooughan
    fieeercean
      imal.

She pronounced *lily* "leely." It was a good idea to lengthen the accented syllables. But she didn't always know which ones they were unless they had a written accent mark. In "soul of a cherub, celestial tongue" there was no way to know. Well, the important thing was feeling because without feeling knowing all the rules didn't matter.

The man
the man with
the man with the heart
the man with the heart of a leely.

It was early when she got to the school, but she still felt discouraged because not many people were in the seats. But she thought in our country people always come late and when would we ever get rid of that habit? On the small stage, behind the improvised curtain, the girls from the Fourth of July School were quietly rehearsing the Barcarolle. The singing teacher was sounding "la" for them very seriously with a little silver whistle that played the single note. When he saw her there, smiling, he greeted her with a smile and stopped waving his arms, but because he was shy, or didn't want to seem servile, or really wasn't, he did not interrupt the rehearsal. She was grateful he didn't, because in that brief time she was going over the poem in her mind and if they interrupted her she'd have to start all over again from the beginning. As if she were really using it, she cleared her throat every five or six lines even though she knew this only irritated it more, just like that teacher whose students, just to annoy him, said his eye was red and he began to rub it and rub it until it was so red they burst out laughing, or like monkeys, if you put a little bit of caca in the palm of their hand they keep smelling it and smelling it until they died. Oh these obsessions! What really made her angry was that she was sure it would be gone when she finished her number. Yes sir. But it was awful in the meantime to think she'd get a frog in her throat right in the middle of the recitation.

It would really be stupid to be afraid of the audience. Even if they didn't like her reading, it wouldn't be because of her but because people in general are very ignorant and don't know how to appreciate poetry. They still had a lot to learn. But that was exactly why she would take advantage of every opportunity to present good poetry to the public and make herself known as a reciter of poetry.

"But Señora," the worried Director General reproached her when he arrived in a sweat. "I was going to pick you up. You shouldn't have come alone."

She looked at him in an understanding way and politely reassured him.

Since becoming First Lady it always made her happy when she had the chance to show she was a modest person, possibly much more modest than any other woman in the world, and in the mirror she had even practiced a charming smile and expression that meant, more or less, "How could you think such a thing? Do you imagine I've become conceited because I'm the President's wife?" But the Director thought he was being treated ironically, and in a state of depression began talking without rhyme or reason about one thing and another. As soon as the other artists had arrived and gathered around her, he took advantage of the opportunity to move away. Later he could be seen, round and plump, giving orders and arranging everything in accordance with the principle that if you don't do things yourself they don't get done.

He only came back to her to say, "Get ready, Señora. We're going to begin."

Since he'd had some practice, the Director explained calmly that they were gathered there moved by a strong feeling of human solidarity. That many children were undernourished, something the Government was the first to regret, as the President told him personally when he called on him to inform him of the fact we must do something for those children for the sake of the great destiny of the nation you move their consciences move heaven and earth move their hearts to support this noble crusade. That many people from all walks of life had already offered their disinterested help and our North American friends that noble and generous nation that we could rightly call the dispensary to the world had promised to make a new sacrifice of cans of powdered milk. That our task was modest at first but we were ready to take every step to turn it into not only a concrete reality in the present but an inspiring example for future generations. That we had the high honor of enjoying the support of the First Lady of the Republic whose exquisite art we would have the privilege of enjoying in just a few moments and whose generous maternal instincts had been moved to tears when she learned of those unfortunate children who because of drunken parents or mothers who had abandoned them or for both reasons could not enjoy in their modest homes the sacred institution of breakfast which endangered their health and impaired their ability to take advantage of the education that the Ministry which we have the honor to represent here tonight was determined to give them convinced that the book and only the book would solve the secular problems which confronted the nation. And I thank you.

After the applause the little girls from the Fourth of July School sang with their usual sweetness the la, lala, lalalalala of the Barcarolle while the pianist waited nervously, impatient to begin his waltzes that like so many other things that day in different parts of the world also began and ended with all happiness and glory.

She bowed her head, saying a silent thank you. She crossed her hands and contemplated them for a moment, waiting for the right atmosphere. Soon she felt that from her mouth and through her words Saint Francis of Assisi was returning to the world—small, sweet, the most humble creature on earth. But then the illusion of humility was left behind because other words, somehow connected to the first, changed his appearance, turning him into an angry man. And she felt that it had to be this way and no other because she found herself warning him of a wolf whose fangs had horribly dispatched shepherds, flocks, and every living creature that crossed its path. Yes sir. Then her voice trembled and she shed a tear at the precise moment when the saint told the wolf not to be bad and why didn't he stop spreading terror wherever he went among the peasants and was he perhaps from hell. Although immediately you could almost see a great peace burst from her lips when the animal, not without having reflected for a moment, followed the saint to the village where everyone was amazed at seeing him so gentle even a child could feed him from his hand. Then the words came out sweet and tender and she thought the wolf could also feed the child so he wouldn't faint with hunger in school. But she was in anguish again because in one of Saint Francis' careless moments the wolf returned to the forest to kill the country people and their flocks. Here her voice took on a tone of implacable condemnation, and she raised and lowered it as needed, forgetting about her cold and her damn nerves of the past few days, just as she had known it would be. On the contrary, a wonderful sense of security, security, security enveloped her, for it was easy to see that the audience was listening to her deeply affected by the barbaric actions of the beast, although she knew that soon, right now, they would change roles and the wolf would become the accuser not the accused, when with his usual confidence Saint Francis went looking for him again to tame him once more. Even if you didn't want to you had to be on the side of the wolf whose words were easy to interpret: Yes, everything was just fine, wasn't it? There I was all tame eating whatever they felt like throwing to me and licking everybody's hand like a lamb while men in their houses gave themselves over to envy and lust and anger and made war on each other and the weak lost and the bad triumphed. She said the words "weak" and "bad" in such differing tones that no one could possibly doubt she was on the side of the weak. And she was sure things were going well and her recitation was a success because she really grew indignant at so much evildoing, it made the wolf's seem small by comparison, after all he was not a rational being. Without even realizing it the time had come when she knew that soon, now, now the words must burst from her throat not too strong, not too tender or furious or gentle but full of despair and bitterness, what else could the saint feel when he conceded that the beast was right and finally turned to Our Father who aaart in heaaaven.

She stood for a few moments with her arms held high. The sweat was streaming between her breasts and down her back. She heard them clapping. She lowered her hands. Secretly she arranged her skirt and modestly she acknowledged their applause. The public, after all, was not so ignorant. But it cost her a great deal to bring them to poetry. That's what she was thinking: little by little. While she shook hands with the people who came to congratulate her, she felt overpowered by a sweet, soft sense of superiority. And when a humble woman came up to greet her and said how nice she was on the point of embracing her but controlled herself and was content to ask "Did you like it?" well, the truth is she wasn't thinking about that anymore but how fine it would be to organize another performance soon in a larger hall, maybe in a real theater where only she would be in charge of the whole program because the bad thing about these little soirées was that the musicians bored the people even though they raved about them in the newspaper the next day, it wasn't fair. No sir.

At the door of her house she invited the Director General and two or three friends in for a drink "to celebrate." She wanted to prolong for a little while the conversation about her triumph. She wished her husband were there to hear what they were saying so he would know she wasn't making it all up. How well everything went, don't you think, and how much do you think we took in?

The Director General informed her very elaborately that they had made a profit of $7.50.

"That's all?" she said.

He thought with bitterness but said with optimism that it wasn't bad for the first time. And they hadn't advertised enough.

"No," she said, "I think it's the hall, it's very small."

"Well, of course," he said. "You're right about that."

"What should we do?" she said. "We have to do something to help those poor children."

"Well," he said, "the important thing is that we've made a start."

"Yes," she said, "but the main thing is to go on. We have to prepare something more serious."

"I believe that if we can count on your help . . ." he said.

"Yes, if we can get a theater just see how I'll recite but it has to be a big theater because if not you see what happens you work hard preparing things and then you don't get anything anyway I'll talk to my husband he's always pushing me to recite it's my greatest joy did you see how the people want to hear poetry if you could've seen what I felt when a woman who doesn't even know me said she liked it very much I think that a poetry recital would be a success what do you say?" she said.

"Certainly," he said, "people like it a lot."

"Look, I'm worried," she said, "about how little we took in today. What if I give you a hundred pesos so it won't be so bad? I really want to help. I think little by little we'll do all right."

He said certainly, that little by little they would do all right.

THE ECLIPSE

When Brother Bartolomé Arrazola felt that he was lost, he accepted the fact that now nothing could save him. The powerful jungle of Guatemala, implacable and final, had overwhelmed him. In the face of his topographical ignorance he sat down calmly to wait for death. He wanted to die there, without hope, alone, his thoughts fixed on distant Spain, particularly on the Convent of Los Abrojos, where Charles V had once condescended to come down from his eminence to tell him that he trusted in the religious zeal of his work of redemption.

When he awoke he found himself surrounded by a group of Indians with impassive faces who were preparing to sacrifice him before an altar, an altar that seemed to Bartolomé the bed on which he would finally rest from his fears, from his destiny, from himself.

Three years in the country had given him a passing knowledge of the native languages. He tried something. He spoke a few words that were understood.

Then there blossomed in him an idea which he considered worthy of his talent and his broad education and his profound knowledge of Aristotle. He remembered that a total eclipse of the sun was to take place that day. And he decided, in the deepest part of his being, to use that knowledge to deceive his oppressors and save his life.

"If you kill me," he said, "I can make the sun darken on high."

The Indians stared at him and Bartolomé caught the disbelief in their eyes. He saw them consult with one another and he waited confidently, not without a certain contempt.

Two hours later the heart of Brother Bartolomé Arrazola spurted out its passionate blood on the sacrificing stone (brilliant in the opaque light of the eclipsed sun) while one of the Indians recited tonelessly, slowly, one by one, the infinite list of dates when solar and lunar eclipses would take place, which the astronomers of the Mayan community had predicted and registered in their codices without the estimable help of Aristotle.

DIOGENES TOO

> Sooner murder an infant in its cradle
> than nurse unacted desires.
>
> WILLIAM BLAKE

As for time, as for distance, what is called the material fact of transporting oneself from one place to another through space, it was certainly very easy for P. (as the Headmaster called him when, strong knuckles and trembling mustache, he reprimanded him) to reach his house. And yet, how difficult! And no, it was not that he was weak or sick. Aside from an imperceptible, hardly bothersome cranial deformation, he was a child like any other.

It was the atmosphere in his house that he disliked, the appearance—I will not call it gloomy, but neither was it pleasant—of the two rooms: their darkness and the fine dust that invaded everything, even his nostrils, making him conscious of his breathing, an indefinable, constant bad smell that floated through every corner, all of this accompanied by his mother's monotonous repetitions: "You should study your lessons, you should study, you should." Reason enough for the simple task of going home to be difficult and hateful.

He noted by way of contrast the joy, the pleasure of his classmates—eight, nine, eleven years old—when, the sun still high, the moment arrived for them to leave the big old house with its narrow classrooms full of teachers—so distant, now, so unreal—whose names he was forgetting or had forgotten as easily as the precise location of colored seas and impossible rivers.

My house—as I think I've already mentioned—was a few blocks, perhaps four and a few steps more, from the school. Maybe five. I can't stay for certain; there's no point in my trying to recall a single time when I took the direct route home. What I used to do, what I always did, what I needed to do, was to make a great detour, like the one that gets you out of the opening paragraphs of this story.

When I left school I generally walked to the markets where I would go into ecstasies when I saw the yellow and red fruit and heard (and learned) the fruit vendors' rough talk, or to the riverbank where you can hear strange, mysterious noises just at sunset, or sometimes to the churches where there were saints (some of them mutilated—I never found out if that is how they were in life or if those defects were due to the effects of time on the material they were made of) and female saints who inspired a raw terror in me that I still feel.

I measured time's passage by waiting until the sun was completely hidden before I approached my house. The door was always open; my mother would open it early—perhaps she never locked it—so I would not interrupt her crocheting when I rang. At the time I didn't know that the hour of sunset changes from day to day. Which was why in June, when the days grow long and it seems they will never end, I would arrive so late that sometimes my mother, worried at what could have happened to me, was waiting at the door. Then she would slap me in a fury and dig her nails into my arms while she scolded me. But despite the blows and the reprimands, I never understood that the sun could move so slowly, and I continued to come home late, sometimes with feet covered in mud and soaked by the lashing rains of summer that in my country is called winter.

It was during a vacation—longed for all year and soon unbearable—that I became fully aware that things were not going very well in my house.

My father was away. I remembered, then I confirmed the fact, he went away frequently. And I had the feeling that although she seemed calmer when he wasn't there, my mother—impossible, impossible!—was lying when she assured me he was working in one city or another in the interior, working so he could bring home lots of gold coins, and—I say this not meaning any criticism—as far as I could see we really needed them. Then I would ask when that would happen, and she would stop talking or change the subject or tell me to study or (with the obvious intention of making me think about something else) scold me for something I had done or failed to do a long time before.

I'm sure I shouldn't say this: The fact is, my father was a bum, what they call a real bum. He was proud of it and enjoyed making his bad reputation even worse; otherwise the neighbors wouldn't try to avoid him anymore.

I don't believe any other child (except my son) has had a father like mine. Can he even be called a father?

For a long time he tried to shake loose my idea that I was his son. I can still see, still hear clearly the same scene repeated many times over in exactly the same way: When everybody was asleep in the old apartment building, he would come home completely drunk, filling the entire apartment with his heavy, exhausted breathing and its disgusting stink of wine and vomit. I close my eyes and see him walking as quietly as he can, like a ghost, his index finger over his lips to show silence while he staggers from side to side without ever losing his balance completely.

A stranger seeing him might have thought he was, to a certain extent, a considerate drunk especially respectful of other people's sleep. But his silence and his gestures, unfortunately, did not reflect those admirable qualities in a drinker. They hid a diabolical meaning instead. His only purpose was to surprise an imagined lover in my mother's room.

It was his obsession at the time. Later I found out that it was not the only one. Once (one time among many) he abandoned our house completely, certain that all of us—my mother, me, the dog—were plotting to kill him in his sleep. Although I subsequently thought that my mother should have done it, his absurd suspicions were unfounded because she loved him.

When he was completely convinced (or so he thought) that once again he had been deceived, that the lover was more astute and less of a night owl than he was, he would come over to the cot where I lay sleeping and take me in his arms, shaking me in his rage, hurting me with his breath and his soft, idler's hands. I would burst into endless screams that could have wakened the entire city. But he was not satisfied until he had hit me for a long time and shouted "You're not my son, you're not my son," as if he wanted to convince the neighbors and convince me, a boy of six, that I was not the child of a mother like other children had but the son of a (I learned the word later) whore.

Mama would finally come to my rescue and take me away from that voice, that alcoholic breath, for which I thanked her from the bottom of my heart. Then I would curl up, trembling with cold, unable to sleep, nervous, frightened, seeing strange things in the darkness for a long time. Usually I sobbed for a while—sometimes without really wanting to—so my mother would feel sorry for me, sympathize with me, and cry a little too.

Because those scenes were repeated so often, I eventually came to believe that my father really wasn't my father. The one thing I couldn't understand was why he would always hit me that way because I was not his son, while it never occurred to him, not even once, to do the same thing to the other neighborhood kids who were surely not his children either.

Except for those times, I hardly ever saw him. He usually got up very late, when I was already in school collapsing with fatigue and not understanding the arithmetical operations that the teacher, who was probably also certain we were not his children, tried to beat into our heads with slaps and punches. Today I am amazed that I endured so much, that I can repeat the multiplication tables although I stammer and tremble uncontrollably.

I come home, my arms full of packages. I throw some of them on the bed; it looks like a huge dining room table covered with a long, smooth, white crocheted tablecloth. There are some plates on it. Big plates full of fruit. But I soon discover they are not plates but enormous flower paintings of (strange) green roses embroidered with brilliant silk thread.

I take off my hat and toss it, and it lands right on the dog's head. He growls and shakes it off. (I look into the dog's eyes; they have a strange glow.) Then, like someone getting ready for a surprise, with my eyes full of mischief, I look at my wife and son (who bears an extraordinary resemblance to me) and from an inside pocket of my jacket I start to remove (pretending all the while to hide it) something that slowly—very slowly—begins to take the shape of a tricycle. My son—I—has always wanted one and why shouldn't I give it to him now that I have plenty of money? Except there must be some mistake, because instead of the necessary, correct, classic three wheels, an infinite number of wheels tumble out one after the other until they fill the room and become annoying, unbearable. I think: a manufacturing defect. Slightly embarrassed, I smile and start to put everything back into my pocket, back where it was before except in reverse. The wheels disappear with a golden metallic ringing sound, but the last ones—which had been the first—go in with great difficulty, oppressing my heart, making my breathing labored, almost suffocating me, choking me as if too large a mouthful of meat were stuck in my throat. I feel the beads of sweat break out on my forehead. I must stop at once. Any more and I'll pass out, destroying the happiness of my wife and son. I am obsessed by the thought that if I die, no one will be able to figure out the tricycle's mechanism, explained only on a piece of paper—or papyrus—that the salesman chewed and swallowed noisily so no one could ever reveal the secret of its construction.

In order to survive I must take out the wheels again, but there's another problem with the mechanism and now they are as resistant to being removed as they were to being returned to their original place. Inspired—inspired—I decide to take off my jacket and throw it far away—or close by, it's all the same. I can't because the sleeves are tied to my shoulders with strong white straps. I don't like the straitjacket. It's an infernal device. I throw myself to the floor. That's not the solution. I kick my legs wildly. I feel cold. I keep my legs still. When I can't stand any more, when I can't stand any less, when I'm drenched with perspiration, I cry and shout with all my might. My wife and son look at me with enormous, embarrassed eyes. My wife—my mother—comes, puts her hand on my forehead, gently wipes away the sweat, gives me a little water—very little water—and explains that it's called a nightmare.

Toward the end he didn't treat me so badly; he didn't even insult me. Just every once in a while he would kick me, not very hard, just when he had the chance.

It took my mother and me several weeks to realize that a new fixed idea had taken control of his thoughts. He no longer looked for lovers under the beds, or smelled the food to see if it had been poisoned (as if he could find that out by smelling it), or smashed the dishes on the floor shouting that they had not been washed properly and he was being treated worse than a stranger. He had found a new victim: dogs.

In fact, day by day my soul was overwhelmed by a deep contempt for those animals. I came to despise them more than anything else in the world.

All the passions I might have nourished otherwise settled into a kind of thick, heavy sediment inside me, leaving behind on the surface, on the first layer of daily living, the disgust, the repulsion I felt toward those servile, humble animals with their teary, gentle eyes, their dripping tongues always ready to lick with pleasure the foot that does them harm.

My first victim (how many others have not yet fallen) was our own dog whose name—too degrading, too doglike*—I do not wish to state here. Come to think of it, I believe his name played a major role in the outcome. Perhaps if he had been called something else, I wouldn't have noticed him. A dog's name is as important as the dog himself. A man or woman can, if they choose, and

*Diogenes

for whatever strange, eccentric reasons, find another name for themselves. It's a question of taste, and with three announcements by the Bureau of Public Records in the newspapers with the smallest circulation, the matter is taken care of. But a dog has to endure his name for his whole life unless he decides to take to the streets and become a bony, nameless stray, but that is a hard, sad life, and few are willing to settle for being thrown out of restaurants and the urinals of bars with a generic "Beat it, mutt!" much less an evil kick to the stomach. I remembered that the ancient philosopher had chosen *can* as the lowest, most despicable thing one could find. And I was happy to admire him for imitating dogs so that men would despise him as much as he despised men. I happened to read in a book: "Once, at a dinner, there were some who threw him bones as if he were a dog and he, approaching them, pissed on them as if he *were* a dog." I also hated the old cynic—so forthright!

Sometimes one has to say monstrous things. What I'm going to say is a little monstrous: I think my father was jealous of the animal. I've reached this conclusion through the association of certain ideas; I can't explain the death of Diogenes in any other way.

In any case, the dog was to blame for much of what happened. Who tells dogs to have that look that's so teary, so tender, so loving? And who told ours to hide under the bed whenever my father appeared? Wouldn't it have been better to go out and greet him (even at the risk of a kick) instead of provoking him with flight that was hopeless? No. He always did the least sensible, the most stupid thing. Sometimes he would start to howl even before my father hit him. It never lasted long. My father couldn't stand it.

It was a hot afternoon. I was diligently reviewing some multiplication tables. My mother was doing her endless crocheting. I can't call her to mind without the silver needle and the little ball of white thread on a newspaper on the floor. I don't know how she took care of her other domestic chores; I can only remember her crocheting or ironing what she had crocheted. The apartment was filled with little doilies that did not beautify the rooms (which was undoubtedly her intention) but gave them a look of vulgar bad taste instead.

Her black metal irons stood in the most surprising, the most absurd places. Her work was also an obsession, I suppose. When she wasn't working she moved her fingers feverishly as if she were actually crocheting without realizing it, as if on no account did she want to lose the rhythm begun who knows how many years ago. If I hadn't grown accustomed to seeing the ball of thread on the floor, I could easily have believed that she produced it herself, like a spider.

The dog had sprawled in a corner, sweating profusely through his tongue and nose.

The brick where he rested his head was covered with vapor at each movement of his lungs. I liked to write my initials with my finger on this vapor, but my mother did not always allow it: "You're a very dirty child."

As I said, he took the three of us by surprise. What we least expected was his arrival or the manner in which he arrived. He came home early, in a very good mood. Sober. Clean. Smiling. Happiness is easy to communicate. He communicated his happiness to all of us. It was a pleasure to have father like him, and for the moment I forgot about his beatings.

He took off his hat and tossed it very gracefully (it seemed to me) onto the hook on the other side of the room.

Then he went over to my mother and caressed her, passing his hand, slowly and gently, over her hair. As he bent down to kiss her he said a few words I couldn't hear or don't remember. But I'm sorry I don't remember because I'm sure they were sweet and kind.

When my turn came he walked toward me, patted me twice on the shoulder, and said with a smile:

"How are you?"

I lowered my eyes, feeling a blush on my cheeks:

"Okay, Papa."

Then he sat down. He seemed a little embarrassed. We hadn't seen him for several months (or years). He obviously wanted to talk, to keep saying pleasant things, but he remained quiet, his eyes half-closed or looking at the beams (a little dirty with smoke, it occurred to me) that supported the ceiling.

My mother offered him something, or simply said something.

She stood up to close the window only when it began to grow dark and a cold breeze blew into the room. Then she returned to her work in silence.

We could all hear it clearly when the dog began to growl the way they do when they feel a heavy stillness. He lay in the corner like a lizard, his four paws stretched out and his belly flat on the floor, as if the heat were still excessive.

When I heard him I moved my eyes slowly in my father's direction. He was smiling. My mother was looking at him too. When she saw him smile she smiled. When I saw her smile I smiled. Then we all looked at the animal again at the same time, and he smiled too in his way. What relief I felt when I heard my father break the silence again by drumming his fingers, clearly intending to call Diogenes over to him.

When he called, the dog began to move slowly, dragging himself, pushing himself with his hind legs. He never expected to be treated with so much affection. I imagine even the dog realized that my father was not drunk as usual, that this day was different.

To make him lose his fear completely, my father continued to call him with whistles and affectionate diminutives: "Here, doggy doggy."

That day I had a vague idea of what happiness was like. I saw my mother happy, my father clean and happy, the happiness in the dog's eyes. When he had traveled the entire distance separating him from my father, he was glad. He wagged his tail with extraordinary vigor and let out an occasional growl. For a moment—perhaps he was overdoing it—he rolled over, lay with his paws in the air as if he wanted to show all his pleasure, but he quickly returned to his usual posture; perhaps he was a little embarrassed. My father caressed him with his foot.

Wasn't he partly to blame, not meaning this, God knows, as any criticism? He's dead now, and I should respect his memory, but, knowing my father, how could he have done what he did? I won't swear to it, but it's possible that his only desire was to share his joy. In fact, at a certain moment he turned his head toward me. When he grew tired of looking at me, or when I stopped paying attention to him, he turned his stupid eyes toward my mother and stayed that way for a while, his tongue hanging out, waiting for some word.

That's when my father's expression changed. Very calmly he stretched out his right hand to the table beside him, took one of my mother's irons, and let it fall like lightning on the animal's head. He didn't have a chance to defend himself. He didn't even move. Neither did my mother. Neither did I. There was no need.

Well, you can imagine the next few minutes. When his tail stopped moving, when my father was convinced that he was good and dead, he simply stood up, took his hat, and left. We never saw him again.

Perhaps my husband was not really so bad. I'm inclined to think he was sick, but not all that sick, as he himself would say. His confinement in the sanatorium where I found him, after endless searching, is one small proof among many for saying what I say.

Today he is like a stubborn child, believing that his father torments him because of some imaginary sin committed by his mother before he was born. When this idea disappears from his mind, he'll be cured.

As for me, I say this: One is never free of malicious gossip. And it comes when you least expect it, even from your own children. I hope nobody believes (there are people ready to believe anything, even the most blatant lie) this whole insane story invented with only one evil purpose—to harm me. It's easy to see—and it would be insulting to think no one noticed—that my son begins his lies at the very beginning when he describes himself, knowing very well that he's lying, as a victim of an "imperceptible, hardly bothersome cranial deformation." The truth is that his head is monstrous. It's not my fault. He was born that way. We knew it from the start, when his birth was so difficult.

It is absolutely false that he attended school. He learned to read and write at home.

I am a traveling salesman. The firm of Rosenbaum & Co. can attest to that, and I can show beautiful letters of recommendation, which they were kind enough to write for me, unworthy as I am of their kindness.

My wife died long ago. My son never knew her. He was raised by my mother.

And as far as dogs are concerned, I am sure, I can swear to the fact, that I never killed a single one except for Diogenes. I had to do it. No dog is safe from rabies. Why would he be the exception? At any moment he could have contracted the disease, which, as everyone knows, spreads so rapidly in a geometrical progression that it can quickly kill off entire populations.

If he had been infected by this deadly disease one day, I can't even begin to imagine what would have happened to us all. The consequences would have been unthinkable.

THE DINOSAUR

When he awoke, the dinosaur was still there.

LEOPOLDO (HIS LABORS)

Proudly, almost arrogantly, Leopoldo Ralón pushed the revolving door and once again entered the library in triumph. He looked over the tables with a bold yet weary gaze, searching for a comfortable, quiet place; he greeted two or three acquaintances with his customary resigned gesture that meant "Well, here I am again, back at work," and walked slowly, confidently, making his way with a repeated "Excuse me, excuse me" that his lips did not pronounce but which was easy to discern in his kind and conciliatory expression. He had the good luck to find his favorite spot. He liked to sit facing the street door; it allowed him to rest from his exhausting research each time someone came in. When that person was of the feminine gender, Leopoldo left his book for a moment and looked her over with his usual penetration, with the smoldering look that an alert intelligence can give. Leopoldo liked well-formed bodies, but this was not the principal motive for his observations. He was moved by literary reasons. It's fine to read a lot and study with dedication, he often told himself, but watching people is worth more to a writer than reading the best books. The author who forgets this is lost. Bars, streets, public offices are overflowing with literary stimulation. You could, for example, write a story about the way some people walk into a library, or how they ask for a book, or the way some women sit down. He was convinced you could write a story about anything. He had discovered (and made telling notes on the subject) that the best stories, even the best novels, are based on trivial events, on ordinary occurrences of no apparent importance. The work was superior to the material. Undoubtedly the best writer was the one who created a masterpiece, an object of enduring art, out of a trivial theme. "The writer," he said one afternoon in the café, "who most resembles God, the greatest creator, is the nineteenth-century Spanish realist Don Juan Valera. He says absolutely nothing. Out of that nothing he has created a dozen books." He had made the remark in passing, almost without noticing it. But that statement made his friends laugh and confirmed his reputation as a wit. For his part, Leopoldo made note of those memorable words and waited for the chance to use them in a story.

Once he was certain that no one would dare usurp his claim, he left his papers on the table, stood up, and walked toward the librarian. He took a call card, elegantly removed his trusty pen from his pocket, and in his best hand, carefully and slowly, wrote: E-42-326. Katz, David. *Animals and Men.* Leopoldo Ralón. Student. 32 years old.

For the past eight years he had been subtracting two. For the past eight years he had not been a student.

A short while later Leopoldo was seated again, the book opened at the table of contents as he searched for the chapter that dealt with dogs. Several sheets of white paper and his pen waited impatiently on the table for the moment when they could make a note on some interesting fact.

Leopoldo was a meticulous writer who showed himself no mercy. From the age of seventeen he had devoted all his time to literature. His thoughts were fixed on literature the entire day. His mind worked with intensity, and he never allowed himself to succumb to sleep before ten thirty at night. Leopoldo, however, suffered from one defect: He did not like to write. He read, took notes, made observations, attended conferences, criticized bitterly the deplorable Spanish in the newspapers, solved difficult crossword puzzles as a mental exercise (or for relaxation); his only friends were writers, he thought, spoke, ate and slept as a writer, but he was seized by deep terror when the time came to pick up his pen. Although his constant dream was to become a famous writer, he delayed the moment of realization with the classic excuses: you have to live first, first you have to read everything, Cervantes wrote *Don Quixote* at an advanced age, without experience there can be no art—and other similar arguments. Until the age of seventeen, it had not occurred to him to be an artist. His calling came to him from the outside. He was forced into it by circumstances. Leopoldo remembered how it had all started and thought he could even write a story about it. For a few moments his mind wandered from Katz's book.

He was living in a *pensión*, a high school student in love with the movies and his landlady's daughter. They called her husband "the lawyer" because he had once studied for six months at the Law School. This reason, powerful enough on its own, together with the fact that the other boarders were a doctor, an engineer, a law student, and a gentleman who was always reading poetry, made Leopoldo feel from the very beginning that he was in a particularly intellectual environment.

Leopoldo could not help smiling at this point. He was thinking of a story about his first impulse to become a writer (he would try it for the second time), but his memory of the doctor distracted him. Certainly another good subject.

"R. F., the doctor, had completed his studies nine years earlier but continued as a boarder, undoubtedly because when he became a professional he decided that there were so many people in the building who were likely to fall sick that leaving to search for patients in the street would have been out-and-out folly. Therefore, despite the friendship he claimed to feel for everyone, he never treated anyone free of charge. Consequently, showing a loss of appetite and finding yourself purged were never apart for long; complaining of fatigue and having an ear at your lungs were as close as brothers; displaying signs of fatigue and receiving an injection were one and the same thing. And the good part was that not complaining at all was useless since his motto was that total health does not exist, that feeling absolutely well is worse than having a disease that is known and therefore controllable, and finally, that the cemetery is filled with the overconfident."

Leopoldo took some notes and wrote in his notebook: "Find out if a similar story about a doctor has already been written. If not, think about the subject and work it up starting tomorrow."

He could begin by ridiculing the doctor's professed hatred of surgery and then start in full blast with the time his landlady declared she had appendicitis and needed an operation and the doctor's angry outburst when he heard this. Another of Leopoldo's notes: "For eight days he did not say a word to her after he had announced that he would leave the house if she permitted anything so stupid to happen." Another note: "Treat with irony the fact that when the woman, despite everything, was operated on, he did not carry out his threat but rather, when she came home, tried to convince her that the incision would soon open, which would make his presence indispensable because you never know . . . some dialogue here:

'No, Señora, you must understand. The incision is worse than the disease. The surest way to kill a person is to wound him in the abdomen. Even a child knows that.'

'But I feel fine now. I've never felt better in my life.'

'Señora, you can think what you like, but my duty is to take care of you and prevent a tragic ending.'"

Calm at the prospect of developing this marvel, Leopoldo opened Katz's book and, with no impatience, looked for the chapter on the instincts of dogs. At first, moved by an unconscious desire to avoid his immediate problem, he lingered over the pages that described the pecking order of hens. How strange. One hen pecked the next that in turn pecked the next, and on and on in a succession that ended only because of fatigue or boredom. Leopoldo, with a feeling of sadness, related this distressing fact to the chain of unreciprocated peckings that can be observed in human society. He immediately realized the possibilities this sort of observation opened for writing a satiric story. He made notes. The president of some business calls for the manager and reproaches him for his slackness while he points angrily at a descending graph.

"'You understand better than I that if things go on this way business will fall off. In that case I will be obliged to suggest at the next stockholders' meeting that it would be appropriate to look for a more suitable manager.'

"The manager, stunned by the pecking he has been subjected to, wants to say something but his superior is already dictating and the stenographer is busily recording his words: 'The prosperity observed in our business during the past three months obliges me to think that your threatened resignation is the result not of a natural fear on your part but a mistaken point of view. The fact that sales have declined in the past few days obeys a simple phenomenon observed by Adam Smith, that is, the variability of supply and demand. When the market is saturated . . .'

"The manager then calls the sales manager:

"'You must understand better than I that if things go on this way, etc., I will find myself obliged, etc., more appropriate, etc.'

"The sales manager reacts to the pecking by turning in the direction of the head saleswoman hen:

"'If sales don't go up by twenty percent in the next week, I'm really afraid that you, etc.'

"Missing a few feathers, the head saleswoman pecks at her closest subordinate, who will peck at her boyfriend, who will peck at his mother, who . . ."

In fact, concluded Leopoldo, he could write a good story with this feeble subject. Comparative psychology was something every writer should know about. He made a note that he needed to take notes, and he wrote in his notebook: "THE PECKING STORY. Visit two or three large department stores. Make observations, take notes. If possible, talk with a manager. Get into his psychology and compare it to a chicken's."

Then, before he reached the chapter on dogs, Leopoldo looked carefully at a girl who came in. Now. Here was the chapter. Of course he would transcribe any useful information into his notebook. His tired eyes, encircled by deep blue shadows that gave him an obvious intellectual appearance, ran methodically across the pages. From time to time he would stop, and with a shrewd expression of triumph write a few words. Then the scratching of his pen could be heard throughout the room. His careful hand, covered with fine hair, revealed a strong, persistent character as it traced the letters firmly and decisively. Leopoldo evidently enjoyed prolonging this pleasure.

He had been writing a story about a dog for some seven years. A conscientious writer, his need for perfection had led him to exhaust almost all the extant literature on these animals. In fact, the plot was very simple, very much to his taste. A small dog from the city suddenly finds himself in the country. There, through a series of events that Leopoldo already had clear in his mind, the poor city beast finds himself in the unfortunate situation of having to fight a porcupine to the death. Deciding which animal would be the victor had cost Leopoldo many nights of unrelenting insomnia, for his work ran the risk of being interpreted symbolically by many unprepared readers. If that should happen, his responsibility as a writer became immeasurable. If the dog was victorious, it could be taken as a demonstration that city life did not diminish the valor, strength, desire to fight, or aggressiveness of living creatures when faced with danger. If, on the other hand, the porcupine triumphed, it would be easy to think (hastily, mistakenly) that his story was basically a bitter criticism of Civilization and Progress. And then where would Science be? And railroads, the theater, museums, books, learning? In the first case, it might be thought that he was opting for a supercivilized life removed from all contact with Mother Earth; the triumph of the dog would proclaim that it was possible to get by without her. In that sense a thoughtless resolution could prove awkward for him. Yet God knows nothing could be further from his thinking. He could see the heartless reviews in the newspapers: "Leopoldo Ralón, the Supercivilized Man, has written an ambitious story in which, with unlimited affectation and pedantry, he indulges himself, etc." On the other hand, if the porcupine were to finish off the dog, many would suppose he was maintaining that a wild, hairy animal could overthrow countless years of human striving for a more comfortable, less difficult, more cultured, more spiritual life. For months the dilemma absorbed all his time. For nights on end Leopoldo turned and tossed in his insomniac's bed, searching for the light. His friends found him preoccupied and more haggard and pale than ever. Those closest to him advised that he see a doctor, that he take a rest, but as on other occasions (the story of the interplanetary rocket, the story of the woman under the streetlight in the bitter cold who had to earn a living for her unfortunate children), Leopoldo reassured them with his peculiar resigned air: "I'm writing a story; it's nothing." True, they would have been very glad to see one of those stories completed, but Leopoldo did not show them around. Leopoldo was extraordinarily modest. Leopoldo was not concerned with glory. One day he saw his name in the paper: "The writer Leopoldo Ralón will soon publish a collection of short stories." Only those words between fateful announcements that a movie star had broken a leg and a ballerina was suffering from a cold. But not even this clear recognition of his genius had made Leopoldo vain. So great was his contempt for glory that generally he did not trouble to finish his works. There were times when he did not even bother to begin them. That, too, was not something one could hurry. He had heard, or read, that Joyce and Proust corrected a great deal. Therefore, he usually left a loose detail, some unresolved subtlety, in all his creations. One never knew when one would hit the mark. Talent moved in seven-year cycles of splendor. So often weeks or months had to go by until the right word, as if by its own volition, settled in the exact spot, the one and only indisputable place!

Although Leopoldo might have opted for the death of the dog (after all, there were strong reasons for that too), he finally decided on his triumph. When one thought about it carefully, if he himself wrote with a pen that would not leak in airplanes, if with just a few turns of a disc he himself could communicate with a dear friend across three thousand miles of mountains and valleys, if with a simple request he himself could hold in his hands the work of someone who had written on wax tablets two thousand years ago, and if all this seemed right and proper to him, there came a moment when it seemed perfectly clear that the dog had to win. "Yes, dear, kind animal," thought Leopoldo, "your victory is inevitable. I promise you that you will triumph." And the dog stood on the brink of victory. As soon as Leopoldo finished reading Katz's book, the dog would enjoy his definitive triumph.

But when Leopoldo reached this bold decision, he was confronted by an unexpected difficulty: He had never seen a porcupine.

Then he told himself he had to find out something about porcupines. He thought it absolutely necessary that a porcupine be the rival of his dog. It was more suggestive. The fact that this singular animal was armed with quills had attracted him from the very first. The porcupine shooting its quills would give him the chance to refer, as if in passing, to those human societies, happily now almost completely extinct, which for thousands of years had used arrows to wage war. Not to mention the fact that by displaying a certain cleverness he could find a way to make a veiled allusion to that magnificent response of (who was it? look it up), that arrogant response of X to his enemy's threat that he would obscure the sun with his arrows: "Even better; then we will fight in darkness." Besides, it was obvious that if the dog's rival were a lion (even though this animal was richer in historico-literary allusions), the dog's victory would be somewhat more problematical. It is true he had seen a lion at the zoo, but a lion most definitely would not do. Serpents were a possibility, but they lent themselves to too many theological reminiscences that had to be avoided in a story like the one he intended to write. He already had enough of those with the city-country problem. A spider or some other poisonous insect would be unthinkable. The unfair competition would make the reader lose interest. Clearly it had to be a porcupine. With the porcupine, the chances for defeat, not counting the "we will fight in darkness," were greater and more manageable.

Leopoldo suffered a disappointment when he learned in the book that dogs were less intelligent than most people think. It is true their instinctual development was astonishing, almost as surprising as that of horses who are capable, with some practice, of solving mathematical problems. But intelligence, gentlemen, what we call intelligence—nothing, absolutely nothing. And so he would have to make his hero triumph in accordance with science and not according to his plans, not in the manner he would have liked. He thought sadly that the poor hounded animal could bite the neck of a wild boar but could never ever pick a stone up from the ground and throw it at his enemy's head (he made a note). Yet the way they purge themselves when they feel sick: Didn't that involve an act of intelligence? How many of the people he knew were capable of behaving like that? He remembered the engineer. He could write a story about him. His whole adolescence, if he viewed it carefully, was filled with excellent themes for stories.

The engineer sat at the table beside the doctor. Unlike "the lawyer," he almost never spoke. His manner—silent, not lacking in mystery—could even be used for a good novel. The tale could begin like this, in the most natural way:

"One hot afternoon, when we were beginning our meal, we saw the engineer for the first time. On seeing him, who would have thought that a criminal lurked inside? I remember it all began when the doctor, with his usual solicitude, told the engineer that he was somewhat disturbed by the color of his eyes:

'I don't want to alarm you when you have honored us with your presence in this house for barely two days. Absolutely not. But as your friend and as a professional, it would weigh heavily on my conscience later if I did not warn you in time of the disease I see in your weary eyes. Allow me to say, sir, that you have problems with your liver.' "

Then leave the dialogue to recount in detail the various stages in the hatred that developed between them. For the engineer never allowed himself to be intimidated or prescribed to, and this the doctor could not forgive. If the engineer became sick he did as dogs do: He stopped eating. And if he felt worse he would go to the pharmacy himself, ask for a purge, and take it without saying anything to anybody and without anybody being aware of it except for his frequent and silent nocturnal trips down the hall. "Damn it, what a good story!" Leopoldo said to himself. And he saw, as if it had been yesterday, the doctor's hatred for the engineer and how, with irritating frequency, he predicted his imminent death, never imagining that his own was so near.

And then tell how the engineer always stayed in his room where he was tirelessly designing (this was surely the cause of his eye irritation) a subterranean tunnel for the Canal of La Mancha and a subterranean canal for the Isthmus of Tehuantepec. To conclude, let some time pass and gather them all together in the living room for a family party. The doctor would be late. The engineer too. Then, with simplicity, describe how he was discovered in his room holding a blood-stained knife and staring fixedly (he made a note—like a hypnotized chicken) at the corpse of his enemy lying face down in a frightful pool of very red blood.

Unfortunately, Leopoldo could not resolve his story by having the dog purge himself out of pure instinct or defeat the porcupine by stabbing him. His dog enjoyed all the signs of good health. The problem lay in having him fight with no other weapons but his own, in having him fight to the death with an animal he was seeing for the first time. This produced his usual low spirits and depression. At every turn there were pitfalls that kept him from completing his story. He had gone through whole libraries searching for information about dogs. And now, when he thought everything had been well documented, he realized he hardly knew anything about porcupines. There was no end to it: today a doubt, tomorrow another hesitation. He had to undertake another extensive investigation into the habits of porcupines: their way of life, their instincts, whether they are capable of defeating a dog or if they always succumb to a canine bite, their greater or lesser degree of intelligence. He wondered in despair if this theme, as had been the case on other occasions, had already been used by other story writers, a fact that would destroy his efforts of so many years with one blow, but he consoled himself with the thought that even if the story had already been written, nothing prevented him from writing it again, like Shakespeare or León Felipe who, as everyone knows, took themes from other writers, reworked them, gave them their personal touch, and turned them into first-class tragedies. He thought that, in any event, he had gone too far to turn back now after so many years of constant labor. Not too long ago he had seen—not without bitterness—how his neighbors exchanged knowing glances each time he announced he was writing a story. They'd soon see whether or not he was writing. Could they possibly be right? He blushed. Without realizing it, step by step, he had entered a labyrinth of appearances which he knew perfectly well he must escape if he did not want to go mad. And the best way to get out was to face the problem, to write something, anything, which would justify the circles under his eyes, his pallor, and his announcements of works that were always imminent, always just about finished. Impossible, after all that, to say in the end: "Well, I'm giving it up. I'm not a writer. Furthermore, I don't even want to be a writer." No, he had made a commitment to himself, and now he could not put it off. He had to prove to Leopoldo Ralón that his vocation was not a mistake, that he really was a writer and really wanted to be one. That was the first time he had thought of telling how he had decided to enter the republic of letters. He had turned to his diary and read:

Tuesday the 12th

Today I got up early but nothing happened to me.

Wednesday the 13th

Last night I slept all night. When I got up it was rayning so I have no adventures to right in my dear diary. Just that around 7 there was a tremor and we all ran out to the street but being it was raining today to we got a little wet. Now dear diary I will say goodbye until tomorrow.

Friday the 15th

Yesterday I forgot to right down my adventures but being I had no adventures it does-nt matter. I hope tomorrow I get ahold of 50 cents I want to see a picture they say is very good and the bandit dies at the end.

Saturday the 16th

This morning I went out with a book under my arm to sell it and see if I could get the 50 cents. I was allmost there when

> I met Don Jacinto the man who livs here and I was very embarassed being he reads alot Im going to right this because its an adventure when he saw me with the book he said so you like literature. It made me very embarassed and I said yes. Then he kept on asking questions and I kept on answering. And do you like to right my young friend? I said yes I right all the time. And what do you right pomes or stories. Stories. Id like to see sum. But no there very bad Im just begining. Come come dont be modest Ive noticed a grate deal of talent in you and Ive observed for a long time that you right alot. I said just a little. When will you show me one? When I finish the one Im doing now. It must be very nice. Its OK. Today I will tell everyone at the table that among us there is a great unnown righter, at dinner he told everyone at the table that I was an unnown righter and it made me very embarassed and I said yes. Tomorrow Im going to start to right a story its easy I just have to imagine something and right it and make a good copy. I couldnt see the movie but Juan told me everything from the middle on being he got there late he told me they kill the bandit at the end. I should erase everything I rote today thats no adventure I didn't have any adventure today.

This was how his writer's vocation had been born. From that day on he took notes all the time, he invented plots for movies, plays, detective and mystery stories, love and science fiction stories, in first person, in indirect style, in epistolary or in diary form, with dialogue or without, bloodcurdling stories found in a bottle on a beach or, sometimes, peaceful descriptions of cities and customs. But the moment for picking up the pen moved further away as the years passed. He made notes on facts and themes, he observed and thought deeply everywhere, all the time, but the truth is that despite his undoubted vocation he almost never wrote. He was never satisfied and never dared to think of any work as finished. No, no need to hurry. Among his friends his reputation as a writer was assured. This comforted him. One of these days he would surprise them all with the masterpiece they were waiting for. His wife had married him because she was attracted in part by his reputation. She never saw anything by her husband published anywhere, but she more than anyone was witness to how he had a box full of notes, how he was always filling his pen with inspirational blue ink, how his imagination was always working, how he was always saying he could write a story about anything, even the most trivial incident.

One day the need to prove to himself that he really was a writer drove Leopoldo to begin a story. After allowing his unconscious mind to work all night, Leopoldo awoke one morning and was inspired. It occurred to him that a fight between a dog and a porcupine was a splendid subject. Leopoldo held on to it and gave himself over to the task with frenetic intensity. But he soon realized that it was much easier to find themes than to develop them and give them form. Then he told himself that what he lacked was culture, and he began a voracious reading of everything he could get his hands on, especially anything about dogs. After some time he felt relatively confident. He prepared a good amount of paper, demanded quiet throughout the house, put on a green eyeshade to protect his eyes from the harmful effects of electric light, cleaned his pen, made himself as comfortable as possible in his chair, chewed his nails, looked intelligently at a patch of clear sky, and slowly, interrupted only by the beating of his impassioned heart, he wrote:

"There was once a very pretty dog who lived in a house. He was a good breed and therefore was rather small. His owner was a very rich man with a beautiful ring on his little finger who had a country house, but one day he felt like spending a few days in the country to breathe clean air he was not feeling good being that he worked very hard at his business that was in fabrics and so he could buy good rings and go to the country too, then he thought that he had to take the little dog if he did not take care of him the maid would neglect him and the little dog would suffer he was used to being cared for carefully. When he reached the country with his best friend who was the little dog being that he was a widower the flowers were very pretty it was spring and in that season the flowers are very pretty being that it is their season."

Leopoldo was not lacking in critical sense. He knew his style was not very good. The next day he bought a rhetoric and a grammar. Both confused him even more. Both taught how to write well but not how to avoid writing badly.

The following year, however, with fewer preparations, he was ready to write:

"The dog is a noble and beautiful animal. Man has no better friend, not even among men, where one encounters with painful frequency both disloyalty and ingratitude. In an elegant and well-situated mansion, in a large city, there lived a canine. Of a good breed, he was rather small but strong and extremely brave. The owner of this generous animal, a rich and powerful gentleman, owned a country house. Fatigued by his many important duties, he decided one day to spend some time at his rural retreat, but concerned with the treatment his dog would receive during his absence at the hands of unsupervised servants, the kind and prosperous industrialist took the grateful dog with him. Yes, he feared that the coarse servants would make him suffer because of their indolence and neglect.

The countryside is very beautiful in spring. In this sweet season there are brightly colored flowers in abundance, with dazzling corollas to delight the eye of the dusty pilgrim, and the mellifluous chirp of the happy and trusting little birds is a feast for the delicate ear of the thirsty traveler. Oh Fabius, how beautiful is the countryside in spring!"

He had learned his rhetoric and his grammar well.

Out of danger with regard to this important point, Leopoldo reached the moment when the beautiful and noble animal had to confront the porcupine. He had already covered more than one hundred thirty-two pages with his firm, clear writing; it is true that of these he had sacrificed some fifty-three. He wanted his work to be perfect. His desire was to include everything in that simple theme. His speculations concerning time and space cost him no less than six months of study. His prolonged digressions concerning who is the better friend of man, the dog or the horse, concerning life in the country and life in the city, concerning the health of the body and the health of the soul (not to mention his novel translation of the aphorism *mens sana in corpore sano*), concerning God and concerning dogs without masters, concerning the howling of dogs at the moon, concerning the courting habits of animals, concerning dogsleds and concerning Diogenes, concerning Rin Tin Tin and his times (the dog ascending to the sublime heights of art), concerning fables and concerning who really wrote those attributed to Aesop along with the countless variants that this name has supported in Spanish cost him more than two years of fruitful labor. He yearned to make his work a subtle mixture of *Moby Dick*, *La Comedie Humaine*, and *Au Recherches du Temps Perdus*.

That was some months ago.

At the time in which we find him, he had changed his mind. Now he was in favor of synthesis. Why write so much if everything, absolutely everything, can be expressed in the sobriety of a single page? Convinced of this truth, he had begun erasing and cutting mercilessly, with complete faith in his new artistic direction and, quite often, with an elegant spirit of sacrifice.

On the day we saw him go into the library, his work, considerably reduced, had taken this form, give or take a few words:

"He was a good dog. Small, happy. One day he found himself in an environment that was not his own: the country. One morning a porcupine . . ."

Leopoldo closed Katz's book, where he had found nothing about porcupines. He asked for another book that studied them but was told that, unfortunately, very little had been written about them, so for the moment he had to content himself with the uncertain information contained in the *Little Illustrated Larousse:*

"**Pig** (*Lat. porcus*). Hog; domesticated pachyderm mammal. *Fig. & fam.:* dirty, gross man: *To behave like a pig. Porcupine*, rooting mammal of North Africa whose body is covered with quills: *the porcupine is harmless, nocturnal, and feeds on roots and fruits. Amer.* coendú. *Prov.* Every pig has his St. Martin's Day, everyone must suffer eventually. The best acorns to the worst pig, those who least deserve it are often the most fortunate. The pig is a valuable animal: all parts of its body are edible. The meat, which should always be well cooked, can be preserved with salt. The fat, still attached to the skin, produces bacon; melted down, it constitutes lard. The bristles or hairs of the animal are used for brushes and brooms. Raising pigs is simple and quick; If there are no acorns, chestnuts, and potatoes, of which it is very fond, this animal is content with refuse of any kind."

"Tomorrow," Leopoldo said to himself, "tomorrow I will take a trip to the country for documentation."

A trip to the country! What a beautiful story he could write!

THE CONCERT

In a few minutes she will elegantly take her place at the piano. With an almost imperceptible nod she will receive the thundering homage of the audience. Her dress, covered in sequins, will shine as if the light were reflecting the accelerating applause of the 117 people who fill this small, exclusive room where my friends will approve or reject—I never know which—her efforts to reproduce what I think is the most beautiful music in the world.

I think, I don't know. Bach, Mozart, Beethoven. I'm used to hearing it said that they are incomparable, and I myself have come to imagine that they are. And to say they are. I would much prefer not to find myself in this position. In my heart of hearts I am certain I don't like them, and I suspect that everybody sees through my false enthusiasm.

I have never been a lover of the art. If my daughter had not decided to be a pianist, I would not have this problem now. But I am her father and know my duty and have to hear her play and help her. I am a businessman and feel happy only when I am handling money. I repeat, I am not an artist. If there is an art to accumulating a fortune and controlling the world market and wiping out the competition, I claim first place in that art.

The music is beautiful, of course. But I don't know if my daughter is capable of recreating that beauty. She herself has her doubts. Frequently, after concerts, I have seen her cry despite the applause. On the other hand, if someone applauds without enthusiasm, my daughter has the ability to discover him in the crowd, and that is enough to make her suffer and then hate him passionately forever after. But it's not often that someone applauds without feeling. My closest friends have learned to their sorrow that unfeeling applause is dangerous and can ruin them. If she did not indicate that she considered the ovation sufficient, they would keep applauding for the rest of the night because each of them is afraid to be the first to stop. Sometimes they wait for me to grow tired before they stop applauding, and then I see how they watch my hands, afraid to begin the silence before I do. At first they fooled me, and I thought they were sincerely moved: Time has not passed in vain, however, and at last I know them for what they are. A constant, growing hatred has overwhelmed me. But I myself am false and deceitful. I applaud without conviction. I am not an artist. The music is beautiful, but basically I don't really care if it is or not, and it bores me. My friends are not artists either. I like to humiliate them, but otherwise I don't care about them.

But the other ones irritate me. They always sit in the front rows, writing constantly in their notebooks. They receive free passes that my daughter writes out with care and sends to them personally. I despise them. The journalists. Of course they are afraid of me, and often I can buy them. But the insolence of two or three of them knows no limits, and from time to time they have dared to say that my daughter is a terrible performer. My daughter is not a bad pianist. Her teachers assure me of that. She has studied since she was a child, and she moves her fingers with more freedom and agility than any of my secretaries. True, I rarely understand her performances, but I am not an artist, and she knows that very well.

Envy is a hateful sin, and this vice in my enemies may be the hidden reason for the occasional bad review. It would not surprise me if one of those who is smiling now, and in a few moments will be applauding, in fact originated the adverse criticism. Having a powerful father has both helped and hindered her. I ask myself what opinion the press would have of her if she were not my daughter. I can't help thinking that she never should have had artistic ambitions. They have brought us nothing but uncertainty and insomnia. But twenty years ago nobody would have ever dreamed I would be where I am today. We will never know for certain, she and I, what she really is, how good she really is. For a man like me, the question is ridiculous.

If she were not my daughter, I confess I would hate her. When I see her walk on the stage, a persistent anger boils in my chest—anger toward her and toward myself because I allowed her to follow such an absurd career. She is my daughter, of course, and for that very reason she has no right to do this to me.

Tomorrow her name will appear in the papers, and the applause will multiply in print. She will swell with pride and read to me the laudatory opinions of the critics. But as she comes to the final ones, perhaps those in which the praise is most admiring and exalted, I will see how her eyes fill with tears, how her voice weakens to a faint murmur, how, in the end, she cries, disconsolately and endlessly. With all my power I will feel unable to make her think she really is a good pianist, that Bach and Mozart and Beethoven would be completely satisfied with her ability to keep their message alive.

Now there is the sudden silence that always precedes her entrance. Soon her long, harmonious fingers will glide over the keys, the room will fill with music, and once again I will suffer.

THE CENTENNIAL

"Which reminds me," I said, "of the story of the ill-fated Swede, Orest Hanson, the tallest man in the world—in his time. These days the record he set is frequently broken.

In 1892 he made a well-deserved tour of Europe to display his height of eight feet, one inch. The journalists, with the imagination that distinguishes them, called him the Giraffe Man.

Imagine. Since the weakness of his joints made any effort almost impossible, in order for him to eat, one of his relatives had to climb to the branches of a tree and place special little meatballs, with small pieces of beet sugar for dessert, into his mouth. Another relative tied his shoes for him. And still another was always on the lookout for the moment when Orest would need to pick up some object that by accident or because of his peculiar clumsiness had slipped through his fingers and fallen to the ground. Orest looked at the clouds and allowed himself to be waited on. His kingdom, in fact, was not of this world, and you could see in his sad, distant eyes a persistent nostalgia for earthly things. In his heart of hearts he felt a special envy for dwarfs, and he always dreamed of trying with no success to reach doorknobs and of breaking into a run as he used to in the afternoons of his childhood.

His fragility reached incredible extremes. When he walked along the street, each step made even the Scandinavians fear a spectacular fall. In time his parents showed signs of a greedy pragmatism that deserved the harshest criticism; they decided that Orest would go out only on Sundays, preceded by his Uncle Erick and followed by the servant Olaf, who passed his hat for the coins that sentimental souls thought they were obliged to pay for that show of gravitational danger. His fame grew.

But it is true that happiness is never perfect. Little by little, an irresistible love for those coins began to filter into Orest's childish soul. His genuine passion for minted metal eventually caused his downfall and proved to be the reason for his strange end, as you will see in due course.

Barnum made him a professional. But Orest did not feel the artistic vocation, and the circus interested him only as a source of money. His aristocratic spirit, however, could not bear the smell of the lions or the fact that people pitied him. He said goodbye to Barnum.

At the age of nineteen, he measured seven feet, eleven inches. Then came a period of quiescence, and it was not until the age of twenty-five that he reached his full height of eight feet, one inch, which he maintained until his death. This is how the discovery was made. Invited to London by the gracious command of their British Majesties, he went to the English consulate in Stockholm to obtain a visa. The English consul, being the man he was, received him with no great show of surprise, dared to ask his height and weight, and doubted he was eight feet tall. When the measuring stick revealed that his height was eight feet, one inch, the consul made the serene gesture that means "I told you so." Orest said nothing. He went to the window in silence and spent long moments bitterly contemplating the rough sea and calm blue sky.

From that time on, the curiosity of European monarchs increased his income. In a short while he became one of the richest giants on the Continent, and his fame reached even the Patagonians, the Yaquis, and the Ethiopians. In the magazine that Rubén Darío edited in Paris, you can see two or three photographs of Orest smiling beside the most celebrated personalities of the time—graphic documents that the great poet published on the tenth anniversary of the artist's death in a homage as deserved as it was posthumous.

Suddenly his name disappeared from the newspapers.

But despite all the plotting and scheming to keep secret the causes that contributed to his unexpected end, we know today that he died tragically in Mexico during the Centennial Celebration, which he attended as an official guest. The causes were twenty-five fractures suffered when he bent down to pick up a gold coin (a "centennial," as a matter of fact) which the obscure Chihuahuan, Silvestre Martín, henchman of Don Porfirio Díaz, threw at him in an outburst of vulgar patriotic enthusiasm.

I DON'T WANT TO DECEIVE YOU

The first part of the program did not go as planned. In the crowded auditorium an impatient, excited audience moved restlessly in their seats. At the center of the stage stood a microphone, from which an anguished humming occasionally could be heard.

Suddenly a metallic voice announced over the loudspeaker that the film's actors, just arrived from France, would be on stage to say a few words and (this was not mentioned although it was the best part) to show themselves in the flesh. The master of ceremonies, a diligent bald man, a mixture of timidity and confidence, assumed a certain professional tone when he spoke that immediately revealed his lack of experience.

As if everything had not been arranged ahead of time, the female star showed great surprise when she was called from her box, but she soon came on stage in all her radiance and said thank you very much to wide applause. Then the male lead appeared and, after a brief silence in which he could not find anything better to say, shouted in bad Spanish "Viva México!" and received a tremendous ovation.

Then the supporting cast was introduced and, of course, a number of people who had nothing to do with anything, among them a short man who confessed proudly that he could imitate radio actors and animals and then proceeded to do so. Finally, as if they had unfortunately been overlooked, the producer of the film and his wife were presented to the audience.

The master of ceremonies introduced each person with intrepid praise, and requested applause for all of them. He was not very skilled, but he hid his ineptitude by extolling everyone and moving his arms frantically as he asked for the applause that the public was less and less willing to grant him.

"We also have with us," he announced finally, "the wife of the producer, that great actress"—urgently he consulted a scrap of paper—"that great actress Señora Fuchier, who is going to say a few words and let's give her a big hand!"

Eight or ten people in the boxes responded wearily to his feverish clapping.

As she approached the microphone, Señora Fuchier had an opportunity to show off her blonde beauty and her shining dress and her jewels. Uncertain and awkward, she turned a little knob nervously for several seconds until she managed to raise the microphone to mouth level; she gave a wry smile as if to say "Finally!" and the audience smiled with her in sympathy.

"My dear public, thank you very much," she began. "First of all, I want to say that I'm not a great actress as my dear friend Señor, Señor . . ."—and she pointed at the master of ceremonies—"has just stated. I'm not even an actress. Of course I'd like to be one and give you frequent moments of happiness but, well, I think art is very difficult and frankly, well, I mean, I shudder at the very idea of being in front of a camera with the lights aimed like they were going to shoot me. I guess it feels like that. So really I don't know why he insists I'm a great actress. Imagine, not just an actress but a great actress. I really wish it was true because in spite of everything, well, I feel a great attraction for the stage. At school, many years ago now, we had a group and put on some very pretty pastorales, you can just imagine, but I could never get over my shyness and as soon as I was in front of an audience I could feel my thoughts going I don't know where and I would break into a sweat because I realized everybody was staring at me like I was naked and then I didn't even know whether I was playing a shepherdess, a sheep, or Baby Jesus. You can imagine. When I forgot my lines, forgot what I was doing there, what I did was make up something and talk and talk about any old thing just so I wouldn't stand there like an idiot and not say anything. Well that's why I'm asking you not to think that a real, full-fledged artist is going to speak to you."

Scattered applause and murmurs of impatience and approval could be heard in the auditorium. A thin man turned to his wife and whispered, "Well, what do you think of this one?"

"I just want to say how happy I am to be here with you tonight but between that and being a great actress, well, I mean, that's far from the truth. I'll say! If my husband Señor Fuchier didn't run the company, well, I don't think I'd even be here. Besides, when he insisted that I bring to life on the silver screen the character in *Winds of Liberty* that we're going to see now, I remembered what happened at school and I said to myself, 'Now what? Suppose you can't?' And the more he urged me with his constant 'Go on, do it, in the movies you don't have to know how to act,' I took it as a remark about my lack of artistic talent, I mean, he didn't believe in me and I never wanted to do it because I know how I am. As a matter of fact I really do like acting and sometimes when I'm alone at home I stand in front of the mirror and without anybody knowing because I'd be too embarrassed I try out a few of the pastorale parts just to stay in practice. I forget about everything, and I'm happy. But if somebody comes in and sees me reciting I pretend I'm combing my hair or trying to kill a fly. What I'd like to do most is comedy. It's easier because if you run into a wall, well, I mean, the audience laughs and pays no attention. In drama it's another story."

The more respectful in the audience managed to quiet the sounds that could be heard throughout the auditorium. The impatient resigned themselves to listening to Señora Fuchier a little while longer with a mixture of amusement and confusion. Only the thin man insisted on making noise with his newspaper, but his wife said to him, "You're impossible!"

"There were times when I wanted to start studying. But no, I never dared to. I wanted to, sure, but 'Now what?' I asked myself, and I'd spend the whole day thinking maybe tomorrow, maybe tomorrow. This is what I want to make clear because I don't like to give myself credit where credit's not due. You're all very good to me but between that and my being in the service of Thalia, who's the muse of theater, well, there's an enormous gap."

The urgings to be reasonable were ignored by most of the audience, and the clapping started up again, this time louder and mixed with whistles. A shout from the amphitheater mimicked Señora Fuchier's voice, and everyone laughed, thinking it belonged to the man who did imitations of radio actors and animals.

"In the first place you have to study a lot and I'm no good, I mean, I've never been any good at studying because I'm easily distracted. Like they say I lose the thread and start thinking about something else and can't concentrate. And the thing that art requires more than anything else is concentration and long hard work and not thinking about anything else. That's it, I told myself, what you need is commitment. The fact is you don't have a calling. It's true you like the theater but not all that much so why even start? Suppose you can't? If it's to please your husband, and you know how much he loves you, then fine, but if it's just vanity why even start? That's what I tell myself when I think about it at night, and I guess that's what my husband thinks too. Who knows? You won't believe it but in my heart it always makes me feel a little like crying."

The master of ceremonies, alert to his responsibilities, looked at everyone and gestured in his urgency to explain: "What can we do? It's not my fault. I realize it's a sad situation, but I can't do anything about it."

"I've come to this microphone, well, I mean, because I want you to know how happy I am to be here tonight with such great artists but between that and what this gentleman here said, well, the truth is I don't want you to get the wrong idea about me. If I could promise you I'd try, I'd study and try to be worthy someday, you know, of the name of actress, but for now I have to be honest and not deceive myself or you."

Meanwhile, worried about his own problems, the master of ceremonies kept trying to make himself understood with gestures and knowing glances. He wanted to give the public this message: "You must understand. It doesn't seem right just to cut her off. Maybe if you clap louder, or whistle louder, or something, of course I'm the master of ceremonies but this is all so peculiar. Can you understand my situation? Only once, some years ago, did I have an experience like this. Well, it was when I was just starting out and was easily embarrassed. One day the President of the Republic came to my town, and by coincidence an uncle of mine was celebrating his birthday, and when he saw the President he thought he had come to town to congratulate him and began to tell him over the microphone that he didn't deserve the honor and was not worthy of the President's coming to see him, and I didn't know how to get out of it. Well, what do you want me to do, I'm sorry too. Her being a great actress, well, I mean, I was just being polite."

"I want to repeat, you know, how happy I feel to be here tonight for the opening of this festival of Italian cinema. It suddenly occurs to me that maybe it would be easier for me to work in a neorealist film but I tell myself 'What now? What if you're no good?' I don't know, maybe that's the way I should go: a simple part with no complications, you know, where I wouldn't be afraid to improvise a little and let my personality go. Oh I don't know."

The gestures of the master of ceremonies grew more and more desperate. He wrung his hands and winked his eyes, but a careful observer would have understood that somehow his uncle was involved again with the President of the Republic.

A moment arrived when the audience no longer knew where to direct its attention—to Señora Fuchier talking about her aspirations, her fears, her self-justifications, or to the master of ceremonies with his bewildered gesturing. It opted for open laughter and foot stamping. The thin man gave free rein to his instincts and tried to stand on his seat, but his wife pulled him down by his sleeve and said, "What's the matter with you?"

"Maybe if I studied with a good teacher I could get used to audiences and concentrate because what I need most is concentration and art, you know as well as I do, what it requires is concentration."

One by one, the other guests of honor had skillfully maneuvered their way off the stage. Señor Fuchier went to the projection room and told them to start the picture. Then, against a moving musical background, you could see the shadows of the master of ceremonies and Señora Fuchier, one on each side of the stage, running around and waving their hands and making their final explanations.

COW

While I was traveling on the train the other day, I suddenly stood up, happy on my own two feet, and began to wave my hands with joy and invite everyone to look at the scenery and see the twilight that was really glorious. The women, the children, and some gentlemen who interrupted their conversation all looked at me in surprise and laughed; when I quietly sat down again, there was no way for them to know what I had just seen at the side of the road: a dead, a really dead cow moving past slowly with no one to bury her or edit her complete works or deliver a deeply felt and moving speech about how good she had been and all the streams of foaming milk she had given so that life in general and the train in particular could keep on going.

COMPLETE WORKS

Professor Fombona had devoted forty of his fifty-five years to a selfless study of the most diverse literatures, and in the best intellectual circles he was considered a first-rate authority on a wide variety of authors. His translations, monographs, prologues, and lectures, without being what might be termed works of genius (at least, that is what his enemies said), could, under certain circumstances, constitute a precious record of everything that had ever been written, especially if the circumstances were, let us say, the destruction of every library in the world.

He had achieved comparable glory as a teacher of the young. His select group of avid disciples, with whom he usually shared an hour or two in the afternoon, saw in him a humanist of unbounded erudition, and followed his suggestions with an unquestioning fanaticism that alarmed Fombona himself more than anyone; he had often felt the weight of their destinies as a heavy burden on his conscience.

Feijoo, the most recent, had made a timid appearance. One day, under some pretext or other, he had dared to join them in the café.* Accepted first by Fombona, he then became part of the group as every good neophyte does—with a fear he could not hide and a reluctance to participate in the discussions. After a few days, however, when his initial shyness had been overcome to some extent, he decided to show them some verses. He preferred to read them himself, stressing with an annoying schoolboy intonation the sections he thought most effective. Then he folded his papers with nervous calm, put them in his briefcase, and never spoke of them again. When confronted by any opinion, favorable or unfavorable, he displayed a controlled, irritated silence. It goes without saying that Fombona did not think the works were good, but he saw in the author a hidden poetic force struggling to get out.

Feijoo's lack of confidence could not escape Fombona's feline perceptions. He thought about him often and was on the point of giving him a few words of praise (it was obvious that Feijoo needed them), but a strange reluctance he did not understand, or tried by every means to hide from himself, prevented his saying those words. On the contrary, if anything at all occurred to him it was a joke, some witticism about the verses that invariably provoked everyone's laughter. He said it "cleared the air" and made his presence as a teacher less evident, but bitter remorse always overcame him immediately afterward. Moderation in praise was the virtue he cultivated with greatest care, undoubtedly because at Feijoo's age he was ashamed to write poetry, and an invincible blush—the more he fought it, the more difficult it was to conquer—reddened his face if anyone praised his tentative compositions. Even now, when forty years of tenacious literary activity—translations, monographs, prologues, and lectures—had given him a security he had not known before, he avoided any kind of praise, and the flattery of his admirers was, for him, a constant threat, something he secretly pleaded for but always rejected with a shy or superior gesture.

In time, Feijoo's poems began to show noticeable improvement. Of course, Fombona and his group did not tell him so, but when

*Daysie's, on Calle Versalles, near Reforma.

Feijoo was not there, they commented on the possibility of his becoming a great poet. Finally, his progress was so evident that Fombona himself grew enthusiastic, and one afternoon, very casually, he told him that *in spite of everything* his verses were really quite beautiful. Feijoo's blush at the unexpected praise was more visible and painful than ever. He obviously was suffering because of the future demands these words implied: As long as Fombona had remained silent, he had nothing to lose; now he was obliged to surpass himself with each new effort in order to maintain his right to that generous statement of encouragement.

From then on it became increasingly difficult for him to show his work. On the other hand, from then on Fombona's enthusiasm turned into a discreet indifference that Feijoo could not understand. A feeling of impotence overwhelmed him, not only when he was with the others, but even when he was alone. Fombona's praise was a little taste of glory, but the risk of criticism was something Feijoo did not have the strength to face. He was one of those people who is harmed by praise.

The coffee is not very good at Daysie's, and recently the air has been polluted by television. Let us not linger over an unpleasant description of that banal atmosphere, which is not to the point, not even for the sake of seeing the animated faces of the adolescents at the tables, much less for listening to the conversations of the somber bank clerks who, with the gentle melancholy of their profession, like to talk at twilight about numbers and the subtly perfumed women they dream about.

Iturbe, Ríos, and Montufar were discussing their respective specialties: Quintilian, Lope de Vega, and Rodó. In the heat of the coffee that the talk had allowed to cool, Fombona, like the conductor of an orchestra, indicated each one's correct note and, from time to time, extracted from the bottomless pockets of his gray jacket (cruelly damaged by layers of stains of a not very mysterious origin) cards with new information by means of which posterity would know there was a comma that Rodó forgot to write, a verse that Lope practically found in the street, a turn of phrase that infuriated Quintilian. Every eye shone with the joy that these erudite contributions invariably awakened in people of a sensitive nature. Letters from fundamental specialists, notes from distant friends, even contributions from anonymous sources all added, week by week, to the exhaustive knowledge about those great men, so far apart in time as well as space. This variant, that simple erratum discovered in the texts, increased the group's faith in the importance of their work, in culture, in the destiny of the human race.

Feijoo, as was his custom, arrived silently and immediately took his place at the edge of the conversation. Although he knew Lope (although "knowing" Lope de Vega was something deemed impossible by Fombona), it was unlikely he could determine with any clarity the precise difference between Quintilian and Rodó. It was easy to see he felt annoyed and somehow diminished.

Fombona considered the moment propitious. As was his habit in such cases, he produced a heavy silence that lasted for several minutes. Then, smiling a little, he said:

"Tell me, Feijoo, do you remember the quotation from Shakespeare that Unamuno uses in the third chapter of *The Tragic Sense of Life?*"

No, Feijoo did not remember it.

"Look it up; it's interesting; it might be useful to you."

The next day, just as he expected, Feijoo mentioned the quotation and his poor memory.

Unamuno stopped being a topic of conversation for several days. And Quintilian, Lope, and Rodó had time for considerable growth.

When Unamuno had been completely forgotten:

"Feijoo," Fombona said again, smiling, "you who know Unamuno so well, do you remember which of his books was first translated into French?"

Feijoo could not really remember.

They did not see him on Saturday or Sunday, but on Monday Feijoo had the information, as well as the date and publisher.

On that memorable day, Feijoo was the new guest who contributed to the symposium. Now the conversation improved, and one gray afternoon, when the rain set a vague sadness on everyone's face, Feijoo pronounced for the first time, in clear, distinct tones, the sacred name of Quintilian. Feijoo, the loose piece in that harmonious system, had finally found his precise place in the mechanism. From then on, they were united by something they had not shared before: the desire to know, to know with precision.

Once again Fombona enjoyed the pleasure of feeling himself a teacher, and day after day he made his mark on that impressionable material. Feijoo's indecision was so compatible with Unamuno's! The subject had not been chosen by chance. The field was inexhaustible: Unamuno the philosopher, Unamuno the novelist, Unamuno the poet, Kierkegaard and Unamuno, Unamuno and Heidegger and Sartre. A writer worthy of someone devoting his entire life to him—worthy of having Fombona guide that life and make it an extension of his own. He imagined Feijoo in a sea of papers and notes and galleys, free of his fear, his terror of creation. What security he would gain. From now on that dear, timid boy would be able to face anyone and talk about everything through Unamuno. And he saw himself forty years earlier, suffering in shame and solitude because of the verse that would not come, and when it did, produced only the fiery blush he could never explain. But the old doubts returned to torment him. He asked himself again if his translations, monographs, prologues, and lectures—which constituted, under certain circumstances, a precious record of everything of value that had ever been written—were enough to compensate for the spring he saw only through others, for the verse he never dared to recite. The responsibility for a new destiny weighed on his shoulders. And something like remorse, the old, familiar remorse, began to disturb his nights: Feijoo, Feijoo, dear boy, escape, escape me and Unamuno, I want to help you escape.

When Marcel Bataillon visited us a few months ago, Fombona suggested organizing an event to honor him and his books.

At the small gathering, Bataillon was intensely interested in the new poets, literary research, painting, everything. At about half past ten, Fombona took Feijoo by the arm (he thought he detected a slight resistance that was overcome more by the authority of his smiling glance than by any pressure), approached the distinguished visitor, and stated slowly, calmly:

"Maestro, I would like you to meet Feijoo. He is an Unamuno specialist and is preparing a critical edition of the *Complete Works.*"

Feijoo shook his hand and said two or three words that were almost inaudible but meant yes, pleased to meet you, while Fombona greeted someone across the room, or looked for a match, or something.

PERPETUAL MOTION 1981

Life is not an essay, although we
attempt many things; it is not a story,
although we invent many things;
it is not a poem, although we dream
many things. The essay about the
story about the poem about life is
perpetual motion; that's it exactly,
perpetual motion.

I wish to change my style and my words.

LOPE DE VEGA

FLIES

There are three themes: love, death, and flies. For as long as man has existed, this emotion, this fear, these presences have always been with him. Let others deal with the first two. I concern myself with flies, who are better than men, but not women. Years ago I had the idea of compiling a world anthology of the fly. I still do.* I soon realized, however, that it was a practically infinite undertaking. The fly invades all literatures, and, of course, wherever one looks one finds the fly. No true writer passes up the opportunity to dedicate a poem, a page, a paragraph, a line, to the fly; and if you are a writer who has not yet done so, I advise you to follow my lead and begin immediately; flies are the Eumenides, the Furies; they punish. They are the avengers of something, we don't know what, but you know they have pursued you on occasion and, as far as you can tell, will go on pursuing you forever. They watch. They are the vicars of an unnameable being that is exceedingly good, or

* Throughout this book you will see
a small, absolutely inadequate sample of the anthology.

else malevolent. They hound you. They follow you. They observe you. In the end, when you die, it is both probable and sad that a fly will suffice to carry your poor distraught soul off to somewhere. Having inherited the task *ad infinitum,* flies transport the souls of our dead, our ancestors, who in this way can remain close to us, be with us, protect us. Our tiny souls transmigrate through flies, and flies accumulate wisdom and know everything we dare not know. Perhaps the final transmitter of our ungainly Western culture will be the body of this fly, reproduced but not enriched over the centuries. As I believe Milla said (an author about whom you know nothing, naturally, but because he was concerned with the fly, you hear his name mentioned for the first time today), the fly, if viewed correctly, is not as ugly as it appears at first sight. But, in fact, it does not seem ugly at first sight precisely because no one has ever seen a fly at first sight. Every fly has *always* been seen. There is some doubt as to which came first, the chicken or the egg. It has never occurred to anybody to wonder whether the fly came before or after. In the beginning was the fly. (It was almost inevitable that in the beginning was the fly or some phrase like it would appear here. We live by sentences like these. Fly-sentences, which like fly-sorrows, mean nothing. The pursuing sentences that fill our books.) Forget about that. It is easier for a fly to land on the nose of the Pope than for the Pope to land on the nose of a fly. The Pope, or the King, or the President (the President of the Republic, naturally; the president of a financial or commercial firm, or of the company that manufactures product-x, is generally foolish enough to consider himself superior to flies) are incapable of calling out their Swiss guards or royal guards or presidential guards to exterminate a fly. On the contrary, they are tolerant; at the most, they might scratch their noses. They know. And they know that the fly also knows and watches them; they know that what we really have are guardian flies who constantly keep us from falling into great, authentic sins, the kind that require true guardian angels who may suddenly grow careless and become accomplices, like Hitler's guardian angel, or Johnson's. But never mind. Back to noses. The fly that perched on your nose today is a direct descendant of the one that landed on Cleopatra's. And once again you fall into the ready-made rhetorical allusions that everybody has used before. You make literature in spite of yourself. The fly wants you to envelop him in an atmosphere of kings, popes, and emperors. And he succeeds. He controls you. You cannot speak of the fly without feeling disposed to grandeur. Oh, Melville, you had to sail the seas before you could finally set that great white whale on your desk in Pittsfield, Massachusetts, not realizing that Evil had long ago circled your strawberry ice cream on the warm afternoons of your childhood; and, with the passage of the years, flew over your head at twilight when you tore occasional hairs from your golden beard as you read Cervantes and polished your style; and did not necessarily inhabit that misshapen vastness of bone and sperm incapable of harming anyone unless that person interrupted his siesta, like mad Ahab. And Poe and his raven? Ridiculous. Just look at the fly. Observe. Think.

Linnaeus might have said that three flies can
consume a cadaver as quickly as a lion.

HENRI BARBUSE, *HELL*

PERPETUAL MOTION

Pape: Satan, pape: Satan Aleppe

DANTE, *INFERNO*, VII

"Did you remember?"

Luis became involved in a complicated but basically weak mental effort to remember what it was he was supposed to have remembered.

"No."

Juan's gesture of disgust indicated that this time it must have been something really important and his having forgotten would bring the usual negative consequences. It was always the same. The whole night thinking I mustn't forget only to forget at the last minute. As if he did it on purpose. If they only knew the effort it cost him trying to remember, let alone remembering itself. Just like elementary school: 9 × 7?

"What happened?"

"What do you mean what happened?"
"Just what I said. How could you forget?"
He didn't know what to say. An attempt at counterattack:
"Nothing happened. I just forgot."
"I just forgot! And now?"
"And now?"
Resigned and conciliatory, Juan ordered, or according to Luis afterward, perhaps he simply said that they wouldn't discuss it anymore and did he want a drink.

Yes. He helped himself. Whiskey and water. He put in three ice cubes that began to melt rapidly in the heat, although not enough to make him decide to put in another one. It had a soothing amber color. Why soothing? Not of course because of the color but because it was whiskey, whiskey with water that would make him forget he had to remember something.

"Cheers."
"Cheers."
"What a life," said Luis ironically, shifting in the wooden chair and looking calmly at the beach, the ocean, the boats, the horizon—the horizon that was even better than the boats and the ocean and the beach because out there you didn't have to think or imagine or remember anything anymore.

On the oblivious sand several bathers were running in the last light of dusk with their soft hair and their bodies darker than tan after several days of daring exposure to the severity of the sky king. Juan watched them thoughtfully. He was thinking, palely, that Acapulco was no longer the same, perhaps he was no longer the same either, only his wife was the same, and the one certainty was that right now she was embracing another man behind some rocks or in some bar or on some boat. He didn't really care, but that didn't mean he didn't think about it all the time. The two things had nothing to do with one another. Julia would go on being Julia forever, just as he had first seen her six years ago when, without provocation and with some surprise on his part, she stared at him at a party where he hardly knew anyone and came up to him and asked him to dance and he said yes and she put her arms around him and began to excite him rubbing up against him and searching for him with her legs and moving against him gently but with calculation so he would feel the brush of her breasts and stop being nervous and not be afraid.

"Would you like another one?" said Luis.

"Thanks."

And as soon as she could she kissed him and encircled him and led him away and introduced him to her friends and got him drunk and that same night, when they didn't even know each other's last names, when they were in her apartment at three thirty in the morning and he didn't even have time to defend himself she pulled him into bed and possessed him in such a way that when he realized she was a virgin he wasn't even surprised though she controlled everything that year and the second, third, and fourth year of their marriage. He couldn't say she had anything else—not beauty or talent or money—she had nothing but that.

"The ice doesn't last at all," said Luis.

"Not at all."

Nothing, nothing at all.

Julia came in wearing slacks, her hair still wet from the shower.

"Aren't you going to offer me a drink?"

"Sure. Help yourself."

"How nice."

"I'll get it for you," said Luis.

"Thanks. Did you remember?"

"He forgot again. Can you believe it?"

"That's enough. I forgot and so what?"

"Aren't you two going to the beach?" she asked.

She drank her whiskey with pleasure. No need to be cruel.

The three of them were silent. Don't speak or think about anything. How many more days? Five. Four counting from tomorrow. Nothing. If only you didn't have to see anybody. Well, maybe not that. Well, who knows. The thing was to get used to it. They're all suntanned. Dark, dark.

When dark night spread its blanket they asked for another bottle and more water and ice and then more water and more ice.

They began to feel good. Really good. The stars were twinkling a distant blue when Julia suggested going to the Guadalcanal to eat and dance.

"They have two bands."

"Why not four?"

"Okay?"

"Let's get dressed."

When they got there they saw it was too early for the Guadalcanal, just as Juan had said. A few scattered gringos drinking sadly and dancing seriously, animatedly, in boredom. And a few of us, much too drunk too early. But at about one o'clock people started to come in, and soon, if you'll pardon the metaphor, there wasn't room for a pin. In obedience to tradition, Julia invited Juan and then Luis to dance, but after two numbers Juan didn't want to anymore and Luis was not very good (he said he forgot the steps, forgot if it was a mambo or rock). Then, as she had for one, two, three, four years, Julia found someone to have a good time with. It was easy. All she had to do was look a certain way at the men sitting alone at other tables. It never failed. Soon some young man would come over (a national, one of us) and seeing she was blonde would ask her if she would care to dance, and she would answer looking not at him but at her husband, asking permission that she knew ahead of time he would not deny, and she would stand up and stretch her arms toward the man who more or less laughing would begin his rapid excuses for mistaking her for an American and then, really disconcerted, would laugh when she told him yes, in fact she was an American, and for a while he would be self-conscious since it was obvious she had lived in the country for many years making it utterly ridiculous to try to begin the conversation again with the well-worn had she been in Mexico long and did she like Mexico. But then she would raise his spirits with the never failing tactic of pressing her legs against him so he would understand this was a matter of dancing not of asking questions or tormenting himself in an effort to find things to talk about, since if it was true that feeling physical pleasure was good, what she liked best was to be carried away by the thought that her husband would be suffering as usual knowing she was in another man's arms or imagining that with this one she would use exactly the same tactics she had used with him and at this moment he would be full of resentment and anger and have another drink and after two more he would turn his back to the dance floor so he would not see the maneuver he knew by heart and they would come to the table at prudent intervals with more distance between them than there had to be like two innocent doves and talk almost in shouts and laugh with him and then immediately skillfully move away to lose themselves beyond the most distant couples and embrace to their hearts' content and kiss without saying a word but certain that in a few minutes when her husband was completely drunk they would be safe and the young national could take them all in his car with her in the front seat not close to him at all but in fact more united than ever because his right hand was searching for something between her thighs while she talked in a loud voice about trivial things like the heat or the cold, depending, while her husband pretended to be drunker than he really was with the sole object of letting them do as they pleased and seeing how far they would go, and from time to time he would grunt so Luis would think he was sound asleep and wouldn't think he knew about anything. Then they would reach their hotel and she and her husband would get out of the car and the young national would say good night and offer to take Luis to his hotel and he would accept and they would happily say goodbye at the door until the car pulled away and when they were alone again they would go in and have another whiskey and he would reproach her and tell her she was a whore and did she think he hadn't seen her rubbing up against that idiot and she would deny it with indignation and say that he was crazy and that he was a poor jealous neurotic and then he would slap her face and she would try to scratch him and would insult him in a fury and begin to undress throwing her clothes around the room and he would do the same until they were in bed and using all his strength he would throw her face down and whip her with a belt made especially for the purpose until she wearied of the game and as always would turn over and let him enter sobbing not with pain or rage but with pleasure, the pleasure of being once again with the only man who had ever possessed her, the only man she had never deceived and had never even thought of deceiving.

"May I have this dance?" the young national said in English.

The fly bites with so much force that it pierces
not only the skin of a man but even that of
the horse and the ox; and even causes pain
to the elephant when it penetrates the folds
of its skin and with its proboscis wounds
the beast to the extent that such is possible,
given its size. As for their unions, flies have
a great deal of liberty, and the male does
not immediately withdraw, as the rooster
does, but is joined to the female for some time,
and she tolerates him and even carries him
in her flight and moves about with the male,
and this does not disturb them.

LUCIAN, "IN PRAISE OF THE FLY"

IT'S ALL THE SAME

To say to hell with everything, to turn into a cynic or proclaim oneself a cynic or a skeptic, to renounce Humanity and propose that horses are better than men. Of course, after Swift, one would not be the first to suggest this, but too much talent is needed to do so without becoming merely an embittered man. On the other hand, a writer's problems are not always, as some people like to think, a question of the development or underdevelopment, the wealth or poverty of the country in which he lives. In rich countries or poor ones, under what conditions were written the works of Dostoevsky, Vallejo, Laxness, Quiroga, Thomas, Neruda, Joyce, Bloy, Arlt, Martí?

These things buzz around me like flies, buzz
around in my throat like flies in a bottle.

JAIME SABINES, *POETIC INVENTORY*

REGARDING ATTRIBUTIONS

In the final analysis, behind every writer there hides a timid man. But even the most pusillanimous will invariably attempt, even by the most oblique, unexpected means, to reveal his thinking, to bequeath it to a Humanity waiting eagerly—or so he supposes—to receive it. If specific personal or social reasons keep him from stating his ideas openly, he will make use of cryptograms or pseudonyms. In any event, in some subtle way, he will leave behind the necessary clues so that sooner or later we can identify him. There are those who cast their stone and conceal their hand, like Christopher Marlowe, the English bard who wrote the works of Shakespeare; or like Shakespeare himself, who wrote the works of Bacon; or like Bacon, who wrote the works that the first two published under the name of Shakespeare.

Bacon's timidity is understandable, of course, for he was a member of the nobility, and writing plays was (and still is) plebeian. Why Shakespeare would have calmly allowed his *Essays* to come down to us with Bacon's signature on them is not as clear, unless that was part of their arrangement. As for Marlowe, wasn't he the author of excellent tragedies? Why then did he think it necessary to attribute his sonnets to Shakespeare? But enough of the English.

Among the Spanish, an individualistic, plainspoken people who are not fond, as they themselves say, of pulling chestnuts out of the fire with somebody else's hand, matters have taken a different course. No Spaniard believes that anyone could be named Cide Hamete Benegeli or Azorín; and they are probably the only nation whose authors choose pseudonyms and then do not have the courage to make unqualified use of them, as if fearing that through some sinister turn of events, the world would somehow fail to learn their true identities. And so we see them called Leopoldo Alas "Clarín," or Mariano José de Larra "Figaro." Nothing like a simple Colette or Vercors. Shortly before he died, Juan Ramón Jiménez was pursued by this doubt: "Pablo Neruda; why not Neftalí Reyes? Why Gabriela Mistral and not Lucila Godoy?" We all know who they are, from the author of *Lazarillo de Tormes* to the writer of the humblest anonymous letter that comes to us in the mail. And no one today believes that the author of Avellaneda's *Don Quixote* is anyone other than Cervantes, who in the end could not resist the temptation of publishing the original (and equally good) version of his novel by serenely attributing it to an impostor, even claiming that the false author maligned him when he called him maimed and old, just so Cervantes would have the opportunity to remind us, with humble pride, of his participation in the Battle of Lepanto.

What does one propose with philosophy?
To teach the fly how to escape from the bottle.

LUDWIG WITTGENSTEIN,
PHILOSOPHICAL INVESTIGATIONS

HOMAGE TO MASOCH

What he did when he had just divorced for the first time and was finally alone and feeling so happy to be free again was to spend a few hours joking and laughing with his friends in the café or at a cocktail party at some opening where everybody would laugh uproariously at the things he said and then return at night to what was once again his bachelor apartment and calmly and with slow pleasure begin to move his equipment, first an easy chair that he placed between the phonograph and an end table, then a bottle of rum and a medium-sized blue Carretones glass, then a recording of Beethoven's Third Symphony conducted by Felix Weingartner; then his thick hardcover copy of *The Brothers Karamasov*, Editorial Nueva España S.A., México, 1944; then he would turn on the record player, open the bottle, pour a drink, sit down and open the book to Chapter 3 of the Epilogue where he would read over and over again the part where the boy Ilucha lies dead in the blue coffin with his hands folded on his chest and his eyes closed and the boy

Kolya, learning from Alyosha that his brother Mitya is innocent of their father's death and is still going to die, exclaims passionately that he would like to die for all of humanity, to sacrifice himself for the truth even if it meant being insulted, and then move on to the discussion of where Ilucha should be buried and the words of his father who tells them that Ilucha had asked him to crumble a piece of bread on the earth that covered him so that the sparrows would fly down and he would hear them and be happy in their company and later he himself, when Ilucha is buried, crumbles and scatters a loaf of bread whispering, "Come, come here, little birds, fly here, sparrows," and he breaks down and faints and then revives and begins to cry again and repents of not giving Ilucha's mother a flower from his coffin and wants to run to her with one until finally Alyosha, in an ecstasy of inspiration beside the great stone where Ilucha wanted to be buried, turns to his fellow students and says the words, those encouraging words, about how they will soon separate but whatever the circumstances they must face in life they should not forget this moment when they were good and if some time when they are older they laugh at themselves for having been good and generous a voice in their hearts will say, "No, it is wrong for me to laugh, for this is no laughing matter," and he tells them this in case they become bad but there is no reason for us to be bad, is there boys? and even in thirty years he will remember those faces turned toward him, he loves them all, and from this moment on they will all have a place in his heart, and in a final outburst of enthusiasm the boys, deeply moved, shout together "Viva Karamasov!" The passage developed with a rhythm so well calculated that the vivas for Karamasov ended at exactly the same time as the final chords of the symphony and he began it all over again as far as the rum permitted, especially as it permitted him to finally turn off the phonograph, take a last drink, and go to bed where he would carefully lower his head to the pillow and sob bitterly again for Mitya, for Ilucha, for Alyosha, for Kolya, for Mitya, for Ilucha, for Alyosha, for Kolya, for Mitya.

He spent his life tossing handfuls of flies into
every glass filled with the wine of praise,
enthusiasm, or joy.

FRANCISCO BULNES

THE WORLD

God has not yet created the world; he is only imagining it, as if he were half asleep. That is why the world is perfect, but confused.

You live to the rhythm of my life.
Fly, my mistress, sated now
by your obscene couplings; on the wall now,
bearing your mate on your back. A rotting
summer
boils and rises, and now a tapestry of
maggots thrives, the family
whose legacy I am from this moment on.

RUBÉN BONIFAZ NUÑO, *SEVEN OF SPADES*

THE BRAIN DRAIN

The phenomenon of the brain drain has always existed, but it seems that in our day it is beginning to be thought of as a problem. Still, it is common knowledge, and fairly well established by general experience, that every truly worthwhile brain either leaves on its own account, or is taken away by someone, or is sent into exile. In fact, the first possibility is the most frequent; but as soon as a brain exists, it finds that it can profit from any one of these three events.

Now, it is my opinion that the concern about a possible Latin American brain drain results from a false premise, or perhaps from undue optimism regarding the quality or quantity of our reserves of this raw material. It is only reasonable that we have grown weary of more developed countries making off with our copper or bananas under constantly deteriorating trade conditions; but, as anyone can see, the fear that they will also take away our brains is vaguely paranoiac, for the truth is we don't possess many that are very good. We take pleasure in our illusions, but as the saying goes, the man who lives on illusions dies of hunger. The suspicion that someone longs to appropriate our geniuses implies that we have them and can therefore continue to permit ourselves the luxury of not importing any.

But the situation must be examined more thoroughly.

If in the next general census we manage to come up with two hundred first-rate brains in Latin America, meritorious brains willing to be seduced by the vain temptations of foreign money, we should consider ourselves fortunate, for the time has come to view matters objectively and recognize that our economies will remain in their present deplorable state as long as we continue to export only tin or agave.

The brain is a raw material like any other. It either has to be sent abroad to be refined so that it can return to us one day as a finished product, or we have to transform it ourselves; but unfortunately, as in so many other areas, our equipment is either obsolete, or second-rate, or simply nonexistent.

Since someone might assume that everything said so far has been said in jest, it is worth offering a few examples.

For each cluster of bananas that Guatemala exports, she earns one and a half cents, paid in taxes by the United Fruit Company, and especially useful to the government in maintaining the social stability and police-imposed order that make it possible to produce another cluster of bananas without interference. True, thousands of clusters are exported every year, but it must also be recognized that aside from order, and not taking into account the depletion of the soil on which this crop is raised, the benefits have been fairly meager. What a difference when a brain is exported! It is evident that exporting the brain of Miguel Angel Asturias has brought notable benefits to Guatemala, including a Nobel Prize. Although many other brains have left the country, as far as anyone can tell they have not made a single crack in the nation's structure; on the contrary, the country seems better off without them and is making more progress than ever.

Where, then, should we direct our energies? To producing bananas or brains? For anyone with even minimal use of his own, the answer is obvious.

Let us consider another example.

During the Second World War, and in the years following that conflict, Mexico exported considerable numbers of manual laborers. Although there were some at the time who challenged, on humanitarian grounds, the advantages of this export, or arm drain, the truth is that each one of these laborers contributed an average of three hundred dollars a year to the country by sending money home to their families. Today no one can deny that these remittances were a significant factor in solving the hard currency problems that Mexico faced in recent years, making possible the impressive economic development she enjoys today. If this was achieved through the contributions of simple, humble, generally illiterate campesinos, imagine what the annual export of 26,000 brains would mean. The salary differential between the two groups is close to astronomical. Again we must pose the question: Which is the better export, an arm or a brain?

Let us define the problem, or the false problem, with absolute clarity.

1. No one is taking our brains away; if they are, it is on a very small scale. Whenever they can, our brains simply leave, in most cases because consumption in Latin America is still far from significant.

2. On the whole, our history proves that a fleeing brain is generally more beneficial to the nation than one that remains at home. Joyce did more for Irish literature in Switzerland than he did in Dublin; Marx was more useful to German workers in London than he was in his own country; it is very likely that if Martí had not lived in the United States and in other countries, the Cuban Revolution would not have had so great an ideologue; Andrés Bello transformed Spanish grammar in England; Rubén Darío did the same for Spanish poetry in France; and I would prefer not to mention Einstein and the atomic bomb. Isolated cases? Perhaps, but what cases they are. If Latin America thinks it currently has twenty

brains like these, and does not permit them to escape, it will be taking foolish risks with its future.

3. Then there are the exiles. The only positive contribution that the dictatorial governments of Latin America have made to the region is their expulsion of brains. At times they err in good faith and expel many that do not deserve it; but when they get it right and exile a good brain, they do more for their country than the Benefactors of Culture who turn local talents into national monuments incapable of saying more than one or two sentences that do not bear a dangerous resemblance to clichés, or, at best, to the kind of braying that never offends anyone and sometimes can even make twilight more beautiful.

Finally, if it is true that this concern is well founded, then, as so often happens, the solution lies at hand and no one can see it, perhaps because it conflicts with our economic preconceptions: Let us import two brains for each one we export.

Therefore we entreat God that he free us from God, and that we may conceive of the truth and enjoy it eternally, there where the highest angels, the fly, and the soul are all brothers.

MEISTER ECKHART, *SERMO BEATI PAUPERES SPIRITU*

THE *ENDYMION* REPORT

Alejandro Pareja, an Ecuadorian; Julio Alberto Restrepo, a Colombian; Julio Alberto Murena, an Argentinian; Carlos Rodríguez, a Venezuelan, each living outside his respective country for political reasons, and Federico Larrain, a Chilean and a simple, sentimental traveler, met on January 22, 1964, at ten thirty at night in a Panama City bar, or whatever it is called, where they discovered by sheer coincidence that they were all poets, that they all admired Dylan Thomas, and that together they knew and could do practically everything. Inspired by some of the worst beer in the world, they remembered or discovered some other things, namely that the New York World's Fair was to open in April, that (at about three o'clock) the five of them had enough money to buy a used car, and (close to dawn), for reasons that will be seen later, they should at all costs be in that city on the day of the opening. Then they went to sleep. A week later they had the car, and despite their clouded political records and the fact that they were poets—better or worse than most is not at issue—they also had the tourist permits they needed to head for what would later be called the Iron Babel by the Nicaraguan officer who detained them. They spent little time in Costa Rica because of the ashes erupting from the volcano Irazu; in Nicaragua, logically enough, they were entertained noisily by friends of the poet Ernesto Cardenal and, with more reserve, by General Chamorro Lugo, director of one of the police units, who, after four and a half hours of dialogue, when he was worn out by cleverly quarreling with them about various subjects relating to his Metapensan countryman and, one might say, protected by his father Rubén Darío whose works he proved he knew by heart, sent them with sufficient brutality and escorts to the Honduran border, not without first confessing that as the great man's compatriot he would always think of himself as a friend of Plato and of poetry, but would think even more of his difficult duty; something similar happened to them in Honduras, but Restrepo cleverly softened and even saved the situation by declaring himself a close relative and of course an admirer of the poet Porfirio Barba Jacob, of beloved memory in that country, and by vigorously praising the pines, to which extremes the police chiefs always respond with enthusiasm and sensitivity; in El Salvador, miraculously enough, they were not bothered by any kind of police, but they did receive a surprise visit from a strange man whom the authorities and most of the writers still at liberty persecuted with enthusiasm after those same authorities and writers had awarded him a prize for one of the best short-story collections produced in the country after Salarrué's, but even though they sympathized with him, they never found out whether or not their strange visitor was crazy, since all he did was to laugh at his persecutors; in Guatemala, of course, they were also detained by the police, although to tell the truth it was only because guerrillas had just shot and killed some blood-stained policeman or other as he was driving down a street in the capital, except that here the Chief of the Guards or whoever he was, after the necessary interrogations and with the refined hypocrisy of those people, said that they could continue their trip, that he was a great friend of poetry and of Plato, and that he hated with all his soul this cross (his job, you understand) with which God and the government wanted to punish him; in Mexico they attended a continental conference of poets where there were fewer declarations of friendship for Plato and poetry and none at all for their colleagues (which did not seem very surprising to them) but where they nevertheless had a wonderful time talking in the sumptuous Journalists' Club and reading their poems to each other in the most beautiful park in the city. Once in New York, where they joyously arrived on April 21, the opening day of the Fair, they wasted no time in going to Greenwich Village—more precisely to 557 Hudson Street, the location of the White Horse Tavern where the aforementioned Dylan Thomas was in the habit of getting drunk day after day (a tavern that certainly should not be confused with Woody's Bar and Grill, where Thomas drank the desolation of the eighteen straight and final whiskies that took him directly to *delirium tremens* and from there to St. Vincent's Hospital at Eleventh Street and Seventh Avenue, and from there to the grave—a bar, incidentally, that has since been torn down but in its glory days stood at the corner of Sixth Avenue, also known as Avenue of the Americas, and Ninth Street—and, prior to their ceremonial libation in memory of the poet, they asked permission of the bartender, who turned out to be a friend of Plato, poetry, and of course, poor Dylan, to place in some corner of the establishment a small leather plaque commemorating this simple act of homage to the poet, which was agreed to and effected, and then they paid for their drinks with good cheer and began their trip out of the city, not without first declaring unequivocably to the reporter* and photographer** who invariably happen to be in the right place at the right time that their homage would consist not only of this, but of leaving the city and the country immediately, refusing in particular to set foot in anything that might possibly resemble any world's fair anywhere in the world, but especially one in New York, a city that surely deserved better luck, all of which, illustrated with two pho-

* Benny Albert of *The New York Times* (*Endymion*, May–June 1964).

** Don Mulligan of the Associated Press, ibid.

tographs, can be read in greater detail in the literary magazine *Endymion*, no. 32, May–June, 1964, 14ff., which Walter Alcott and Louis Uppermeyer, friends not only of Plato and poetry but also of the truth, published with great difficulty eight years ago in St. Louis, Missouri, USA.

4 Kan, Precious Jewel, will be the day on
which Katún 5 Ahau declines. It will be the
time when skulls pile up and flies weep
along the streets of the town and at the
resting places along the streets of the town.

THE BOOK OF BOOKS OF CHILAM BALAM

I KNOW YOU, MASK

Humor and timidity generally go together. You are no exception. Humor is one mask and timidity is another. Do not allow anyone to remove both at the same time.

What kept the foolish flies from savoring your
lunch of distinguished fowl was its superb tail.

MARTIAL, *EPIGRAMS*

THE ADVANTAGES AND DISADVANTAGES OF JORGE LUIS BORGES

When I discovered Borges in 1945, I did not understand him; in fact, I was stunned. Looking for Kafka, I found Borges' prologue to *Metamorphosis* and confronted for the first time his world of metaphysical labyrinths, of infinities, eternities, tragic trivialities, and domestic relations comparable to the most carefully imagined inferno. A new universe, brilliant and fiercely attractive. The passage from that prologue to everything Borges has written was, for me and for so many others, something as necessary as breathing, and as dangerous as coming perilously close to the edge of an abyss. Following him meant discovering and descending to new circles: Chesterton, Melville, Bloy, Swedenborg, Joyce, Faulkner, Woolf; it meant renewing old relationships: Cervantes, Quevedo, Hernández; finally, it meant returning to that illusory paradise of the ordinary: neighborhoods, films, detective novels.

And then there was his language. Today we accept it with a certain naturalness, but in those days his Spanish, so tight, so concise, so eloquent, had the same effect on me as thinking that someone was dead and buried and then, without warning, seeing him alive and well on the street. Through some mysterious art this language of ours, so dead and buried for my generation, suddenly acquired a strength and power we thought it had lost forever. Now, it seemed, Spanish could once again express anything with clarity and precision and beauty; one of our own could tell again, and interest us again, in an *aporia* of Zeno, and one of our own (I don't know if this is another again) could raise a detective story to the level of art. We were subjects of resigned colonies, skeptical regarding the usefulness of a language that had been squeezed dry; we owe the restoration of faith in the possibilities of our inescapable Spanish to Borges and his excursions through English and German.

Since we are accustomed to a certain kind of literature, to specific ways of handling a story or resolving a poem, it is not strange that Borges' methods take us by surprise, and from the very first we either accept or reject him. His principal literary device is precisely this surprise. Beginning with the first word in any of his stories, everything can happen. But a reading of all the stories together demonstrates that the only thing that could happen is whatever Borges, possessed of implacable logical rigor, had proposed from the start. For example, the mystery story in which the detective (a victim of his own intelligence, his own subtle plotting) is pitilessly trapped and killed by the scornful criminal; or the melancholy revision of the presumptive work by the Gnostic Nils Runeberg, in which it is concluded, with tranquil certainty, that God, in order to truly be Man, did not incarnate in a superior human being like Christ, or Alexander, or Pythagoras, but in the baser, and therefore more human, vessel of Judas.

When a book begins, as Kafka's *Metamorphosis* does, by proposing: "Gregory Samsa awoke one morning after a restless sleep to find himself in his bed, transformed into a monstrous insect," the reader, any reader, has no other recourse but to decide as quickly as possible on one of two equally intelligent responses: either throw away the book or read to the end without stopping. Knowing that countless bored readers would decide on the comfortable first solution, Borges does not overwhelm us by telegraphing his first punch. He is more elegant, or more cautious. Like Swift, who begins *Gulliver's Travels* by innocently telling us that the protagonist is merely the third son of a harmless small landowner, Borges introduces us to the marvels of *Tlön* by going to a villa in Ramos Mejía in the company of a friend, who is so real that at the sight of an unsettling mirror he happens to "remember" something like this: "Mirrors and copulation are abominable because they increase the number of men." We know that this friend, Adolfo Bioy Casares, exists; that he is a man of flesh and blood who writes fantasies; but if this were not so, merely attributing this sentence to him would justify his existence. The horrifying, realistic allegories of Kafka begin with an absurd or impossible event and then immediately relate all the effects and consequences of this event with calm logic and a realism that is difficult to accept without the reader's prior good faith or credulity; yet one always has the conviction that this is pure symbol, something necessarily imagined. But when one reads Borges' *Tlön, Uqbar, Orbis Tertius,* the most natural response is simply to consider it a rather tedious scientific essay that is attempting to demonstrate, not very emphatically, the existence of an unknown planet. Many people will go on believing this until the day they die. Some may have their suspicions and will ingenuously repeat the words of that bishop, described by Rex Warner, who boldly declared that as far as he was concerned the events narrated in *Gulliver's Travels* were nothing but a pack of lies. A friend of mine was so disoriented by the collection *The Garden of Forking Paths* that he confessed that what attracted him most about the story "The Library of Babel" was the stroke of genius revealed by using an epigraph from *The Anatomy of Melancholy,* a book, according to him, that was clearly apocryphal. I showed him the volume by Burton and thought I had proved to him that all the rest was invented, but from that moment on he opted to believe everything or absolutely nothing, I can't remember which. Factors that contribute to the effect of authenticity in Borges are the inclusion in the story of real people like Alfonso Reyes, presumably real people like George Berkeley, well-known, familiar places, works that may not be readily available but whose existence is in no way improbable, like the *Encyclopaedia Britannica*, to which one can attribute anything; the serene, journalistic style, in the manner of Defoe; the consistent solidity in his use of adjectives, because for countless readers nothing is more convincing than the precise placement of a good adjective.

And, finally, the great problem: The temptation to imitate him was almost irresistible, but imitating him was pointless. Anyone can, with impunity, imitate Conrad, Greene, Durrell, but not Joyce, not Borges. It is too easy, and too obvious.

The encounter with Borges never occurs without consequences, both advantageous and disadvantageous. I have listed some of the things that can happen.

1. You pass him and don't realize it (disadvantageous).
2. You pass him, go back, and follow him for a while to see what he is doing (advantageous).
3. You pass him, go back, and follow him forever (disadvantageous).
4. You discover that you are a fool and have never had an idea that was even moderately worthwhile (advantageous).
5. You discover that you are intelligent, for you like Borges (advantageous).
6. You are dazzled by the fable of Achilles and the Tortoise and believe that it contains the answer to everything (disadvantageous).
7. You discover the infinite and eternity (advantageous).
8. You are concerned with the infinite and eternity (advantageous).
9. You believe in the infinite and eternity (disadvantageous).
10. You give up writing (advantageous).

Between the provocation of hunger and the passion of hatred, Humanity cannot think about the infinite. Humanity is like a great tree full of flies buzzing angrily beneath a stormy sky, and in that buzz of hate, the deep, divine voice of the universe cannot be heard.

JEAN JAURES, "REGARDING GOD"

FECUNDITY

Today I feel well, like a Balzac; I am finishing this line.

It is known that the ancient gentiles worshiped the vilest, most contemptible brutes. The goat was the deity of one nation, the tortoise of another, of a third, the beetle, of a fourth, the fly.

FEIJOO, *CRITICAL THEATER OF THE WORLD*

YOU TELL SARABIA THAT I SAID HE SHOULD HIRE HER AND PLACE HER HERE OR WHEREVER, THAT I'LL EXPLAIN LATER

To the memory of the
Wright Brothers

It was late when the civil servant decided to follow the flight of the fly again. And the fly, as if he knew himself to be the object of scrutiny, took great pains in the programmed execution of his acrobatics, buzzing to himself but always aware that he was a common ordinary housefly, and that among the many possible ways he could shine, buzzing could not compare to the increasingly wide and elegant circles he was flying around the civil servant who, on seeing them, remembered dimly but insistently and as if he were denying it all to himself how he had been obliged to circle around other civil servants in order to reach his present high position, and without making too much noise either, and perhaps with less joy and more somersaults but with a little more brilliance if brilliance is what you could call, with no sarcasm, what he had achieved before and during his ascent to the heights of public office.

Then, overcoming the sultry heat, he went to the window, opened it firmly, and with two or three brusque movements of his right hand and forearm, forced the fly to leave. Outside, the warm breeze gently shook the treetops, while in the distance the last golden clouds sank definitively to the bottom of the afternoon.

Back at his desk, exhausted by his efforts, he pressed one of five or six buttons and, leaning comfortably on his left elbow (thanks to a clever mechanism in the swivel chair), waited to hear

"Yes sir?"

so that he could order, almost at the same time

"Have Carranza come in"

whom he quickly saw half-serious, half-smiling, pushing

the door in

coming in

and then turning his back tactfully to bend over the knob to close the door again with all necessary care so that it would make no noise except the slight inevitable click that doors make when they are closed and, turning around immediately, as he usually did, he heard

"Do you have Payroll C handy?"

and answered

"Not really handy but I can bring it in five minutes; you look exhausted; what's wrong?"

and came back in less than three with a sheet wider than it was blue which the civil servant glanced at, up and down, without enthusiasm, and then raised it to the clear sky as if he wanted to fly away, fly up, fly far, grow smaller and smaller until he lost his tie and his ordinary shape and became a speck the size of a distant airplane which is the size of a fly, and then an even tinier dot, and finally he handed it back to Carranza, his friend and co-worker, who asked him, puzzled, if anything was wrong, and he heard himself answer

"No, tell Señorita Esperanza that tomorrow Señorita Lindbergh is coming in regard to the matter of the vacancy and tell her to send her to Personnel to see Sarabia. You tell Sarabia that I said he should hire her and place her here or wherever, that I'll explain later."

She is so clever that she sees the wind race
and hears flies cough.

J. & W. GRIMM, *ELSA THE CLEVER*

HOMO SCRIPTOR

Direct acquaintance with writers is harmful. "A poet," said Keats, "is the least poetic thing in the world." As soon as you know a writer whom you admired from a distance, you stop reading his works. This happens automatically. As for the works themselves, a sensible idea, and one that is currently being put into practice, is for the best works, or at least the best-known works, which may also be good, to be published simultaneously in various Latin American countries. The very bad ones should be brought out by the State in luxury editions with leather bindings and illustrations in order to put them beyond the reach of the poor and, at the same time, keep the majority of poets and novelists happy.

The fly buzzing around me at this moment: if it sleeps at night in order to begin its buzzing again, or if it dies tonight, and in the spring another fly, emerging from some egg laid by the first, starts to buzz—in the end it is all the same.

A. SCHOPENHAUER, *THE WORLD AS WILL AND IDEA*

UNDER OTHER WRECKAGE

We see this man walking anxiously up and down in front of the door of the transient hotel on Calle París in Santiago, Chile; he watches and suspects. For the last few days he has done nothing but suspect. He has looked into her eyes and suspected. He has noticed that his wife smiles at him in too normal a way, that everything either seems all right to her or doesn't, that she does not disagree with him as much as before or disagrees with him more than before, and he has suspected. Anyone would. That's how these situations are. Suddenly you feel something strange in the air, and you suspect. The handkerchiefs given as gifts begin to be important, and there's always one missing and nobody knows where it is; just like that, nobody knows where it is. Then this gentleman works up his courage and goes to the hotel. He has finally decided to put an end to his doubts by being man enough to wait until he sees them coming out and then trap them, furtive and surely wearing the expression of unconcern that hides their fear of being discovered. And now, while he waits, he has crossed God knows how many times in front of the large, open, main door, walking back and forth mechanically, and it bothers him when he realizes that sometimes he feels almost no anger. Well, perhaps you have gone through this at one time or another and it is indiscreet of me to remind you, to call to mind something you have buried under other wreckage, other illusions, other films, other facts, for better or worse everything has blurred what at one time seemed to be the end of the world and today, as you know very well, you remember almost with a smile. Or you have leaned against the blue wall across the street. He was a tall, good-looking man with graying hair, about forty years old, it doesn't matter. It was summer, he was wearing linen, he was sweating. We watched him from the second-story window of the building across the way. It was fun to spy on the couples who kept arriving. Old men with young girls. Young boys with old women. Young girls with young boys. Never old men with old women, I wonder why. Middle-aged men with middle-aged women, both men and women very calm. Experienced men with all kinds of little maids who were terrified. Liberated men with liberated women who went in laughing freely, happily, what envy we felt. Sometimes we spent a whole Sunday afternoon, Enrique, Roberto, Antonio, and I, watching them come from the side streets and go in. Or not go in. We would make bets. These two will go in. These two won't. You lost or won because the ones you thought would go in, the ones you bet on, would walk right by only to come back and go in after ten steps when you supposed that virtue was going to enjoy one of her most sensational victories but was, happily, defeated. But getting back to this man—how sorry we felt for him. This man was suffering. He nervously watched the falsely confident exit of each couple, fearful they would be the ones he was waiting for and that in a careless moment they would get away from him, lost in the first shadows of twilight as they used to call it. Look how he cranes his neck, how he stands on tiptoe, how nervous he becomes when anyone comes out and how upset when anyone passes in front of anyone leaving. He goes from one corner to the other only to return quickly in a state of agitation. Perhaps he thinks that at this moment they have managed to elude him. It's incredible. The man is beginning to make us feel sorry for him. If this were not our usual game, we would not have had the patience to observe him from this comfortable window for more than two hours (because it's already seven o'clock) with no real interest in what was happening inside. But it does interest him, what's happening inside, and he imagines and suffers and tortures himself and thinks up bloody acts of vengeance at which he stops and trembles, not knowing if from anger or from fear, although in his heart he knows it's anger. And you and your friends from your comfortable vantage point watch and suffer and are not sure what is happening right now with your own wives and maybe that's why this man who could be you, could be all of you, disturbs you so, as the twilight turns into night and the clerks anxious to return, who knows why, to their homes, increase in number and run laboriously for the buses and trolleys that go by, jammed with people. Finally, suddenly, you see in him an agitation that is much more intense, a nervousness, an anguish, and you realize that the supreme moment he has been waiting for has arrived and you quickly turn your eyes again to the door of the hotel and you see that the lovers are coming out and have realized what is happening, that is, he is there, and pretending to be calm they quicken their pace looking back in their minds and walking faster and holding one another by the arm they turn the corner of San Francisco and you come down quickly from your vantage point so you won't miss what is happening and you find the man still on O'Higgins Avenue and you find him distraught, looking around, roughly pushing people out of his way, turning on his heels, searching, looking here and there, anxious, disconcerted, but now certainly tomorrow, or next Saturday, or Monday, or whenever, he will have the chance to watch when he is less distracted, not as slow as he was this afternoon when it probably wasn't them.

Once a fly dancing . . .
Could fill your heart with dreams none other
knew . . .

W.B. YEATS, THE LAND OF HEART'S DESIRE

HOW TO STOP BEING A MONKEY

The spirit of inquiry knows no limits. In the United States and in Europe they have recently discovered a species of Latin American monkey capable of expressing itself in writing, identical, perhaps, to that diligent monkey who, by hitting the keys of a typewriter at random, eventually reproduces the sonnets of Shakespeare. Something like this naturally fills these good people with wonder, and there is no lack of willing translators of our books or ladies and gentlemen of leisure willing to buy them, as they once bought the shrunken heads of Jivaro Indians. More than four centuries ago Fray Bartolomé de Las Casas finally succeeded in convincing the Europeans that we were humans endowed with souls because we laughed; now they want to convince themselves of the same thing because we write.

> The misanthrope: The sun is good only for reviving the flies that suck my blood.
>
> JULES RENARD, *DIARY*

HOW I GOT RID OF FIVE HUNDRED BOOKS

> Poet: Don't make a present of your book; destroy it yourself.
>
> EDUARDO TORRES

Several years ago I read an essay by some English author—I don't recall which one—who told about the difficulties he encountered in getting rid of a parcel of books he was no longer interested in owning. Now, over the years, I have observed that intellectuals often complain that their books eventually force them out of house and home. Some even justify the size of their seignorial mansions with the excuse that they could not turn around in their old apartments because there were so many books. I have not been, and probably never will be, in so extreme a situation, but I never could have imagined that one day I would find myself in the position of the English essayist, struggling to divest myself of five hundred volumes.

I will try to give an account of my experience. Let me say in passing that the story will probably irritate many readers. It doesn't matter. The truth is that at a certain point in your life you either know too many people (writers), or too many people (writers) know you, or you realize that you happen to live at a time when too many books are published. The moment comes when your writer friends have presented you with so many books (excluding the unpublished manuscripts they generously give you to read) that you would need to devote every day in the year to learning their interpretations of the world, of life. As if that were not enough, the fact is that for the past twenty years my passion for reading has been contaminated by the habit of buying books, a habit that, sadly, is often confused with reading. Twenty years ago I was foolish enough to begin visiting secondhand bookstores. On the first page of *Moby Dick*, Ishmael observes that when Cato wearied of life he committed suicide by throwing himself on his sword, and that when Ishmael happened to feel the same weariness, he simply boarded a ship. I, on the other hand, spent many years following the route of secondhand bookstores. When you begin to feel the attraction of these establishments filled with dust and spiritual penury, the pleasure derived from books has begun to degenerate into a mania for buying them, and this in turn becomes pride in acquiring some rare volume that will astonish your friends or mere acquaintances.

How does this process take place? One day you are peacefully reading in your house when a friend drops by and says: "What a lot of books you have!" This sounds to you as if he were saying: "How intelligent you are!" and the damage has been done. You know the rest. You begin to count your books by the hundreds, then by the thousands, and feel more and more intelligent. As the years pass (unless you really are a poor unfortunate idealist) you generally have greater economic resources at your disposal, have frequented more bookstores, and naturally, have become a writer and consequently own so many books you are no longer simply intelligent: At heart you are a genius. This is at the root of your pride in owning many books.

Finding myself in this situation, I mustered my courage the other day and decided to keep only those books that really interested me, or that I had read, or was really going to read. As he consumes his ration of life, how many truths does a man avoid? Isn't his own cowardice one of the most constant of these? How many times a day do you turn to sophistries in order to hide from yourself the fact that you are a coward? I am a coward. Of the several thousand books that I own through inertia, I had the courage to eliminate no more than a scant five hundred, and even that was painful, not because of what they represented spiritually for me, but because of the diminished prestige that ten meters less of filled bookshelves would signify. Day and night, my eyes turned again and again (as the classics would say) to the long rows, selecting and choosing to the point of exhaustion (as we moderns say). What an incredible amount of poetry, of novels, of sociological solutions to the ills of the world! One supposes that poetry is written to enrich the spirit; that novels have been conceived, at the very least, to entertain us; and even, optimistically, that sociological solutions are a guide to solving something. Viewing the situation calmly, I realized that the first (poetry) was capable of impoverishing the richest spirit, the second of boring the most joyful, the third of confusing the most lucid. And yet what careful consideration I gave to discarding any of the volumes, no matter how insignificant it seemed. If a priest and a barber had helped me without my knowing it, would there be more than a hundred books left on my shelves? In 1955, when I visited Pablo Neruda in his house in Santiago, I was surprised to see that he had only thirty or forty books, mainly detective novels and translations of his own work into various languages. He had just donated an enormous number of true bibliographical treasures to the University. The poet allowed himself that pleasure while he was alive—the only time, come to think of it, when one can.

I will not make a complete survey here of the books I was prepared to give away, but there was a little of everything, more or less as follows: politics (in the bad sense of the word, if indeed it has any other), about 50; sociology and economics, approximately 49; general geography and general history, 3; geography and history of specific nations, 48; world literature, 14; Latin American literature, 86, North American studies of Latin American literature, 37; astronomy, 1; rhythmic theories (so that madam does not become pregnant), 6; methods for finding water, 1; biographies of opera singers, 1; indefinable genres (for instance, *I Chose Freedom*), 14; erotica, 1/2 (I kept the illustrations in the only one I had); methods for losing weight, 1; methods for giving up drinking, 19; psychology and psychoanalysis, 27; grammars, 5; methods for speaking English in ten days, 1; methods for speaking French in ten days, 1; methods for speaking Italian in ten days, 1; cinematic studies, 8; etcetera.

But this was merely the beginning. I soon learned that few people were willing to accept most of the books I had so painstakingly bought over the years at so great a cost in time and money. Although discovering that acquisitiveness was not a universal aberration reconciled me somewhat to the human race, it caused its own discomforts, for once I had made up my mind, getting rid of those books became a compelling spiritual necessity. A fire like the one that burned the Library of Alexandria, a blaze to which these recollections are dedicated, is the easiest path to follow, but it seems ridiculous, and even indecent, to burn five hundred books in the courtyard of your house (assuming that your house has a courtyard). Though people accept the fact that the Inquisition burned people, most become indignant at the burning of books. Certain people who are passionate about such things suggested that I donate all those volumes to some public library or other; but so simple a solution weakened the spirit of adventure involved in the enterprise, and I found it a rather tiresome idea; besides, I was convinced the books would serve as little purpose in public libraries as they did in my house or anywhere else. Tossing them one by one into the trash was not worthy of me, or the books, or the garbage collector. My friends were the only solution. But my political or sociological friends already owned the books that corresponded to their fields of specialization, or in many cases, held inimical beliefs; the poets did not want to be contaminated by the works of their contemporaries whom they knew personally; and the erotic book, even stripped of its French illustrations, would be a burden to anyone.

But I don't wish to turn these recollections into a recounting of supposedly amusing false adventures. The truth of the matter is that somehow I found kindred spirits who agreed to take these fetishes home, where they will occupy space that will deprive the children of air and room but provide the parents with the sense of being wiser, and the even falser and more useless feeling that they are the repositories of a knowledge that is, in any case, nothing more than a repeated testimony to human ignorance, or human ingenuousness.

My optimism led me to suppose that when I finished these lines, begun two weeks ago, the title would be fully justified; if the five hundred that appears there is replaced by twenty (a number that is beginning to shrink because several books have been mailed back to me), the title will be closer to the truth.

. . . and also because of the flies, which were performing in my presence, and in their smaller concert, a music that was like the music in the summer house.

MARCEL PROUST, *AU RECHERCHE DU TEMPS PERDUS*

THE MAIDS

I love servants because they are unreal, because they leave, because they don't like to obey, because they represent the last vestiges of free work and voluntary agreements and don't have insurance or contracts, because like ghosts of an extinct race they come, they go into houses, they pry, they poke around, they look into the abysses of our miserable secrets by reading the coffee grounds or the wine glasses or the cigarette butts or simply by introducing their furtive eyes and avid hands into the closets, under the pillows, or by gathering up the pieces of torn paper and the echo of our complaints while they shake out and sweep up our constant misery and the remains of our hate, alone the entire morning singing triumphantly because they are welcomed as annunciations when they appear with the Nescafé or Kellogg's carton filled with clothes and combs and tiny mirrors still covered with the dust of the last unreality they moved through, because then they say yes to everything and it seems that now we will never lack their protective hand, because finally they decide to leave as they came but with a deeper knowledge of all human beings, of understanding, and of solidarity, because they are the last representatives of Evil on earth and our wives don't know what to do without Evil and cling to it and plead with it please not to leave this earth, because they are the only creatures who take revenge for the complaints of our wives simply by leaving, by gathering up again their brightly colored clothing, their things, their jars of third-class cream filled now with the first-class kind, dirtied a little after their unskillful thieveries. I'm leaving, they say, vigorously packing up their cardboard cartons. But why? Because (oh ineffable liberty). And there they go, malignant angels, in search of new adventures, a new house, a new cot, a new laundry room, a new Señora who cannot live without them and who loves them, planning a new life, denying any gratitude for how well they were treated when they were sick and were lovingly given their aspirin for fear that the next day they would not be able to wash the dishes, which is what really wears you out, preparing meals doesn't wear you out. I love to see them come, ring, smile, walk in, say yes; but no, always refusing to face their Mary Poppins–Señora who will solve all their problems and those of their Papas, their older and younger brothers, one of whom raped her when he had the chance, for at night in bed you show them how to sing do-re-mi, do-re-mi until they are asleep with their thoughts sweetly turned to tomorrow's dishes submerged in a new wave of suds from detergent fab-sol-la-si, and you caress their hair tenderly and quietly tiptoe away and turn out the light just before you leave the little maid's room with its unreal outlines.

Unfading moths, immortal flies,
And the worm that never dies.
And in that heaven of all their wish,
There shall be no more land, say fish.

RUPERT BROOKE, "HEAVEN"

SOLEMNITY AND ECCENTRICITY

To the memory of Dr. Atl, eccentric

Not long ago a group of writers and artists in Mexico announced a campaign against solemnity, a campaign, of course, that like many lost campaigns, past and present, was won on the spot. Those who were not solemn (I hastened to place myself among them) laughed more than ever, wherever they were, pointing the finger at things and people. Those who thought themselves solemn declared with a forced smile that they were not, or at least were only when there was no need to be. Since there are no limits to the ambiguity and hypocrisy that surround us, the first group soon found a way to make their rivals believe they were members of the same party, while the second group made the first believe that they had believed them, that in fact it was all a joke and they belonged to their party. Soon no one knew or cared exactly which group he represented. Once again words or definitions had replaced facts, the essence of things was forgotten, and nothing changed. It was also forgotten that each man can defend his ideas jokingly or solemnly, but the ideas are what really matter (in the event he has any) and the manner in which he defends them may be less important. It is said that Christ never laughed and certainly never told a joke. He was extremely solemn. But his ideas cannot be destroyed, or are very difficult to destroy, simply by laughing at them, perhaps because no one follows them. It seems that the weakest part of the struggle against what was called solemnity was, as we shall see, not finding anything better to replace it.

If having won too quickly was one reason for losing this war, another was blithely imagining that the enemy could be defeated by humor, which is not necessarily the opposite of solemnity. The true humorist attempts to make people think, and sometimes even to make them laugh. But he has no illusions and knows he has failed. If he believes his cause will triumph, he immediately ceases to be a humorist. He triumphs only in defeat. The man who thinks he is wrong is usually right. But these are facile paradoxes.

All right, then. It is common knowledge that if a word is repeated rapidly and often, it soon loses all meaning. Perhaps this is what happened to the concept of solemnity. I see now that the war was really being waged against "false" solemnity, which, like every other false thing, is almost certainly imperishable and represents conformity to the established order, fear of ridicule, rejection of the unknown, respectful deference to custom, longing for security, lack of imagination.

Given this definition, what does it mean to be a "falsely" solemn person? There are solemn acts. To behave solemnly when you are not presiding over a solemn act does not mean you are solemn. It means you are a fool. If you are asked the time and you respond with solemnity that it is a quarter past three (and it is a quarter past three) you are not solemn. You are a fool. But there is no need to exaggerate. If you walk with solemnity and are not leading a solemn funeral procession, you are probably a solemn person; but at that moment you might also have been thinking up a good argument against false solemnity. One must not rely on appearances. As Batres Montúfar said:

If I put a reed in water
and see it bend in two
then I say my eyes deceive me
for I know the reed was straight.

Finally, with regard to the other extreme mentioned in the title, I believe that a valid response to false solemnity and foolishness may not be simple humor but every degree of eccentricity, the eccentricity that is usually both solemn and sublime. For example: In the prologue to the 1961 UNAM edition of William Blake's *First Prophetic Books*, Agustí Bartra cites the poet's first biographer, who recorded the following incident: "Butt visited the Blakes one day and found the couple sitting in a small pavilion at the far end of their garden, completely divested of those troublesome coverings that have been in fashion ever since the Fall. 'Come in!' Blake called to him; 'it is only Adam and Eve you see before you.' Husband and wife, in a state of undress, were preparing to recite a few passages from Milton's *Paradise Lost*." It should be noted that as far as we are concerned, simply reading *Paradise Lost* would be considered highly eccentric.

Since we have begun to recall eccentrics, we ought to review certain cases of English extravagance that appeared several years ago in an issue of the magazine *Du*. Perhaps you may all decide to follow their example and wage your own war against "false" solemnity.

Edward Lear, the founder of nonsense, called himself Lord Defender of Gibberish and Absurdity, Great and Magnificent Peripatetic Ass, and Guiding Light of Foolishness. He was born in 1812, the youngest of twenty-one children. The basis of his nonsensical compositions was his play with English words and spelling. He was fascinated by fantastic, extravagant verbal wit, especially combinations of sound and sense. And yet, in addition to its value as entertainment, this kind of literary absurdity represented something more profound for Lear: It constituted an escape valve for the internal conflicts that grew out of his suffering and sorrow. On the other hand, he may have thought he had created the kind of literature worthy of the vast majority of human beings: With very few exceptions (among whom, of course, he counted himself), they were all idiots.

Francis Henry Egerton, Eighth Earl of Bridgewater (1756–1829), felt no love for his neighbor either; but he did love books and dogs. If he ever borrowed a book, he returned it in a special carriage escorted by four servants dressed in sumptuous livery. By the same token, his carriage might be occupied exclusively by dogs shod as elegantly as Egerton himself, who wore a new pair of shoes every day. His table was always set for a dozen of his favorite dogs. His shoes, arranged in meticulous rows, helped him keep track of his age.

Squire Mytton (1796–1894), who from his youth until the day of his death was the incarnation of extravagant absurdity, died of chronic alcoholism after having attempted to lead his horse down the same path. This horse, in fact, was his favorite drinking companion, and he shared many glasses of port with the animal. On one occasion Mytton set fire to his nightshirt in an attempt to cure an attack of hiccups. He soon recovered from the burns only to die of *delirium tremens.* (Following this example is especially recommended to "falsely" solemn people.)

Charles Waterton was the greatest and most ingenious eccentric of them all. He was a naturalist, a first-rate taxidermist, and a highly skilled tree climber. During the summer, he spent most of his time at the tops of the tallest trees in his garden, studying the habits of birds for hours. He delighted in scratching the back of his neck with the toes of his right foot. He was in the habit of walking on all fours under the table when he had guests, barking and growling like a dog. When he decided to take up the study of orangutans, he locked himself in a cage with an enormous representative of the species in order to cultivate a more intimate relationship. It was love at first sight. They embraced and kissed in a rapture of incomparable bliss. This wise man always slept on the floor with a log as his pillow. He would arise at half past three in the morning, spend an hour in the chapel of his house, and then begin the day's scientific work.

Johann Heinrich Füssli (1741–1825) is an example of the eccentric who takes pleasure in everything that may heighten his reputation (the public is always ready to believe anything) for being a singularly dangerous and malicious character. This small man, with his leonine face, led a sober life and possessed uncommon energy for work, but he would startle his visitors by suddenly appearing as a horrible ghost, wearing his wife's sewing basket on his head.

But let us return to our subject. There may be only two things that can make "false" solemnity seem ridiculous (not conquer it, because false solemnity is foolishness, and that is invincible): true solemnity and eccentricity.

La Rochefoucauld defined solemnity as "the body's recourse for concealing failures of intelligence." That's fine, perhaps because it is a solemn phrase, like almost everything this extremely solemn man said.

The important thing is not to be falsely solemn yourself, to let the falsely solemn bury their own, and the authentically solemn ("Solemn," says the Royal Academy, falsely solemn to its very core, "in its fourth meaning, signifies formal, grave, solid, valid") be what they are, courageously and truthfully. Perhaps in a few of them there lies hidden a potential eccentric, unacknowledged until now, and capable of having himself mummified like Jeremy Bentham, whose full-length mummy can be viewed today inside a glass case in the University of London; or as the above-cited magazine adds, the martyr Thomas More, who always considered himself a great wit; or like Robert Burton, the author of *The Anatomy of Melancholy;* or like Laurence Sterne, author of the preposterous *Tristram Shandy* (which the falsely solemn have never dared to translate into Spanish); or finally, like John Stuart Mill, who wrote these words that are more relevant than ever:

"In our day, the mere example of nonconformity, the mere refusal to bend one's knee to custom are a service in and of themselves. Precisely because the tyranny of public opinion is so great that it considers eccentricity ignominious, it is desirable, if only to put an end to that tyranny, for people to be eccentric. Eccentricity has always flourished wherever and whenever strength of character has flourished; and the amount of eccentricity prevailing in a society has generally been proportional to the amount of genius, mental power, and moral value which that society contains. The fact that so few dare to be eccentric today constitutes the greatest danger for our time."

To crush two clods with one fly.

BENJAMIN PÉRET / PAUL ÉLUARD, *PROVERBS*

WINNING THE STREET

An admirer of poetry who lives in San Blas has written to me in the hope that I will pass this information on to you: On the rare occasions when he comes to the capital, he has observed that a specific street, extending for many or only a few blocks but familiar to him for whatever reason, has suddenly had its name changed, which can sometimes cause him great inconvenience; but after careful thought this does not seem quite so illogical, since he has been informed it is now a practice widely accepted by the public—and that, after all, is what matters. And so instead of complaining, he would prefer to offer an idea that he not only dares to consider original, but that would have the further advantage of making, as the saying goes, a virtue of necessity and, at the same time, contributing to the general culture by increasing civic responsibility and notably encouraging creative activity (and even destructive activity, for life, he admits in resignation, is born of the eternal struggle between the forces of Good and Evil) among the citizenry and so, to make a long story short, and to put it as simply as possible, he proposes that when a poet publishes his first book of verse, and if the book is good, his name *ipso facto*, regardless of his wishes, is to be given to one of our longest and most beautiful boulevards (unless it is a main thoroughfare or a side street, which, as we shall soon see, makes implementation of his proposal difficult, for the fact is that these avenues generally are very far from having anything that could bring the slightest poetic notion even remotely to mind), on the condition that if each new book he publishes turns out to be inferior to the first and, in his case, to those that follow, his name will be removed from as many blocks as the Commission that will be created for this purpose shall deem fitting; and if the offense is repeated, from the same number of blocks again; and so on until, if he is not careful, by the end of his life (it is understood, of course, that he would be required by law to publish a book at fixed intervals*) the poet will see his transitory glory in this world extinguished; and, on the other hand, and in view of the fact that just as negligence combined with ineptitude deserves to be punished, so excellence is no less worthy of reward, if at the same time there appears (and this is in no way uncommon) a bad book by another fledgling poet, this poet's name shall be affixed to the first block at the far end of the boulevard; and if, encouraged by this act of generosity, the second poet's published work improves in the years that follow, his name shall be given to the same number of blocks being taken away at the other end from the poet who began brilliantly, so that both the punishment and the reward will be as fair as possible for both of them. Then, in an outburst of enthusiasm, and as if wanting to strengthen his arguments, he adds that even the most superficial consideration of the advantages of this method would be enough to appreciate the decisive impetus it would give, when applied to other branches of art and science, not only to the progress of the nation but to the progress of the entire world, an area where it would soon be imitated, above all if, moving away from the banalities of poetry, the

*Contrary to the idea cherished by some that every poet should be prohibited from publishing a second book of verses unless he can offer convincing proof that the first is sufficiently bad.

system were to be tested if not on the most grave and transcendental, then on the most urgent problems of peace and war; and that it was worth contemplating what would happen if a great London avenue were to be named Mahatma Gandhi where it began and Lawrence of Arabia where it ended, or if a Parisian boulevard bore the name Albert Schweitzer at one end and Dwight D. Eisenhower at the other, and blocks were taken away and added each time one of them won or lost a battle; but, after some reflection, and thought, and more reflection, and more thought, he was fairly pessimistic in this regard, and therefore preferred that we ignore his digression and return, before he took his leave, to the firmer and much more concrete terrain of poetic creation.

If space and time, as sages say,
Are things that cannot be,
The fly that lives a single day
Has lived as long as we.

T. S. ELIOT, "SONG"

HUMOR

Humor is realism carried to its final consequences. With the exception of most humorous literature, everything that man does is laughable or humorous. In war what we do stops being funny because in war man stops being funny. As Eduardo Torres said: "Man is not content with being the stupidest animal in Creation; he also permits himself the luxury of being the only one that is ridiculous."

Our flies know songs
taught to them in Norway
by the *ganique* flies that are
the white goddesses of snow

GUILLAUME APOLLINAIRE,
BESTIARY

PARADISE

Recently he had been coming to his office a little late, very late really but within the limits he thought the system tolerated, placed there precisely so they would not work, would not get in the way, so that he could come in late because, as he gave it some thought, the important thing was not to stay out altogether, to come in, to be there. Then the boy offered him a cup of coffee, which he accepted gratefully, since it was good to feel you were doing something, that you had something to wait for during the next three minutes, even if it was only a cup of bad coffee smelling of old, very old rats. When the secretaries told him that no one had asked for him ("no one" was different from nobody; "no one" of course meant some superior, some boss in the office hierarchy), he felt calm and confident. The morning would go by with no major anxieties, and now it was all a matter of waiting patiently for noon and then one o'clock and then half past two. But this was always an illusion. The hours are hard to chew, and like the boa with its victims it is better to salivate each one slowly, calmly, so that you can swallow it minute by minute, although in the offices you could see clearly that sometimes after each hour there is another, and then another and another, and there are still thirty minutes left over which you finally use up somehow and then you can go. Naturally you can always count on the newspaper, but you can't spend the whole morning reading the paper. But you know your reserves and are certain that someone, the Great Someone, will be there to talk to you. Someone always listens with interest, or at least pretends to, which is no small matter—listens to your problems with interest and says yes when you need someone to say yes and no that's not right when you need someone to disapprove of the way your wife handles money, or your children, or the papers and books you always leave around with that famous characteristic disorder of yours—you always know where everything is as long as they don't straighten your damn desk; or maybe the movies, no, sports, even less, literature, perhaps, but not very deeply since even if you really know about most of the novels that have been written recently, especially in Latin America, which is all the rage, in fact you haven't read them although you know, well, although you think it is your duty as a writer, but after all you can talk about them as if you really had read them, your instincts or a skimming through are enough to know where Cortázar, Vargas Llosa, García Márquez, or Lezama Lima are heading without having to work so hard especially now when not a day goes by without something new being published and there's really no time to read everything, especially those long novels that are complicated intentionally by the authors just to show they know how to do it. Have you noticed? Have you read *Paradiso?* I couldn't. You haven't finished one thing when the next one appears. You've read it? No, you say jokingly, I'm still getting through *Don Quixote*, knowing full well you've never read *Don Quixote*, that it bores you to death as the great Lope de Vega said about Dante on his deathbed. But joking aside, no, the fact is you haven't had time. Then you think with determination that in half an hour, when you leave, you're going to catch up with the Spanish American novel, and you see a perfect world, a kind of Garden of Eden, where you come home and everything is ready and your wife with her pretty pink apron and her smile, that smile that never leaves her face except when she has problems, serves you your supper right away and your children are all sitting around the table quietly with "10"s in conduct and quick as a wink you eat your dessert and go to your room and pick up *Paradiso* and like those swimmers with big batrachian fins on their feet and oxygen on their shoulders God knows how many meters under the water in slow motion and in colors no one has ever seen before you sink into a deep marvelous reading interrupted only by your own impulses, like going to urinate, or scratching your back, or walking downstairs for a glass of water, or putting on a record, or trimming your nails, or lighting a cigarette, or looking for a shirt to wear to the cocktail party this evening, or making a phone call, or asking for some coffee, or looking out the window, or combing your hair, or contemplating your shoes, in short, all those things that make good reading—and life—so pleasant.

Irritable little gnat she was and always would be and
that was why no one could get on with her poking
her nose into what was no concern of hers.

JAMES JOYCE, *ULYSSES*

But I have been losing any resemblance I may once have had to a writer as my economic circumstances have improved too much and my social relationships have widened to the point where I cannot write anything without offending someone I know, or unintentionally flattering one of my protectors and patrons, which means most people.

How large unto the tiny fly
  Must little things appear!—
A rosebud like a feather bed,
  Its prickle like a spear;

A dewdrop like a looking-glass,
  A hair like golden wire;
The smallest grain of mustard-seed
  As fierce as coals of fire;

A loaf of bread, a lofty hill;
  A wasp, a cruel leopard;
And specks of salt as bright to see
  As lambkins to a shepherd.

WALTER DE LA MARE, "THE FLY"

LIVING TOGETHER

Someone who always complains bitterly of the cross he has to bear (husband, wife, father, mother, grandfather, grandmother, uncle, aunt, brother, sister, son, daughter, stepfather, stepmother, stepson, stepdaughter, father-in-law, mother-in-law, son-in-law, daughter-in-law) is at the same time the cross of another person who bitterly complains of constantly having to bear the cross (daughter-in-law, son-in-law, mother-in-law, father-in-law, stepdaughter, stepson, stepmother, stepfather, daughter, son, sister, brother, aunt, uncle, grandmother, grandfather, mother, father, wife, husband) it has been his lot in life to carry; and so from each according to his ability and to each according to his needs.

The air is not so full of flies in
summer as it is at all times
of invisible devils.

RICHARD BURTON

HEIGHT AND POETRY

Dwarves have a kind of sixth sense
that allows them to recognize one
other on sight.

EDUARDO TORRES

Without standing on tiptoe, I easily measure five feet, three inches. I have been little since I was little. My mother and father were not tall either. When I realized, at the age of fifteen, that I was growing into a very short man, I began to do all the recommended exercises, which did not make me taller or stronger but did improve my appetite. And this was really a problem, because at that time we were very poor. Although I do not recall ever going hungry, it is more than likely that I was malnourished for long periods during my adolescence. Certain photographs (which do not always have to be blurred) prove it. I am saying this because it may be true that if I had eaten not more but better food back then, my height would be more respectable now. On my twenty-first birthday, and not a day before, I acknowledged defeat, gave up the exercises, and went out to vote.

Everyone knows that Central Americans, with a few irritating exceptions, do not generally enjoy great height. But regardless of what people say, it is not a racial problem. There are Indians in the Americas who surpass many Europeans in this regard. The fact of the matter is that poverty and the malnutrition that goes with it, combined with other, less spectacular factors, are the reason that my compatriots and I always invoke Napoleón, Madero, Lenin, and Chaplin when we need to prove, for whatever reason, that a man can be very short and still be courageous.

I am regularly the butt of jokes about my meager height, which almost amuses and consoles me because it gives me the feeling that with no effort on my part, and through my deficiency, I am making a contribution to the fleeting happiness of my disconsolate friends. And when I happen to think of it, I too make jokes at my own expense, which later come back to me as the fruits of somebody else's creativity. What can you do? This has become so common a practice that even people who are shorter than I am manage to feel a little taller when they tell jokes about my height. One of the better witticisms calls me a representative of the Low Countries, and there are others along the same lines. I can see how people's eyes shine when they believe I am hearing this for the first time! Then they go home and face the economic, artistic, or conjugal problems that overwhelm them, and feel somehow as if they have the courage to resolve them.

In any event, the malnutrition that leads to diminished stature also leads, no one knows why, to a fondness for writing verse. When I meet someone shorter than five feet, three inches, on the street or in a gathering, I recall Torres, Pope, or Alfonso Reyes, and I sense, or am almost certain, that I have encountered a poet. In the same way that true dwarves tend to be embittered, those of middling height are generally sweet-natured and given to melancholy and contemplation, and paradoxically enough, the muse seems more comfortable in abbreviated, even deformed bodies: the aforementioned Pope, for instance, as well as Leopardi. Whatever traces of a poet Bolívar possessed came from this. It may be true that the size of Cleopatra's nose still has an influence on human history, but perhaps it is no less true that if Rubén Darío had reached a height of six feet, two inches, poetry in Spanish would never have gotten past Núñez de Arce. With the exception of Julio Cortázar, how can one comprehend a poet six feet, six inches tall? Consider Byron, who was lame, and Quevedo, who was knock-kneed; no, poetry does not hop, skip, or jump.

Now I've reached the point I wanted to make.

The other day I happened to see the guidelines for a Central American poetry festival that has been held in the city of Quezaltenango, Guatemala, since 1916. Along with the usual statement of requirements and prizes that one would expect in this kind of competition, these guidelines also set down, I believe for the first time in history, and I hope for the last, the condition that moved me to compose these lines, although I am still uncertain how it should be interpreted.

Clause E of the paragraph entitled "Submission of Work" reads as follows:

"Each work must be submitted with a separate sealed envelope that is labeled with the poet's pen name and the title of the work, and contains a single sheet with the author's name, signature, address, brief biography, and a photograph. Contestants are also requested to indicate on the reverse side *their height in inches* in order to facilitate arrangements for the ceremonial crowning of the Festival Queen and her court of honor."

Their height in inches.

Once again I think of Pope and Leopardi, akin only in their having heard (with bitterness or with sadness) in the small hours following a night of revelry the couples laughing as they passed the rooms each shared with cruel insomnia.

Fearing flies is the reverse side of loving birds.

OTTO WEININGER, *INTIMATE JOURNAL*

CHRISTMAS. NEW YEAR'S. WHATEVER

The cards and gifts you send and receive year after year or that we send and receive with a somewhat foolish feeling that overwhelms you or us but which slowly, because of an interweaving of memories and forgetfulness, you or we stop sending or receiving, like those trains that pass with no hope of ever passing one another again, or rather, now for self-criticism, since the comparison with trains is really not very good because you would have to be a very stupid train not to meet up again with the trains you've met—like those bourgeois drivers who, just because they are who they are, when they drive their cars feel free of something they cannot name if you ask them what it is and once, only once in their lives, meet up with you at a red light and you exchange foolish knowing glances with them for a moment while you discreetly but meaningfully arrange your hair or adjust your tie or check your earrings or take off or put on your glasses, depending on how you think you look best, with the melancholy suspicion or optimistic certainty that you are never going to see them again but nonetheless live that brief moment as if something important depended on it, or perhaps something not so important, that is, those fortuitous meetings, those conjunctions, just to give them a name, when nothing happens, when nothing needs explanation, when you don't need to understand each other, when you shouldn't understand each other, when nothing needs to be accepted or rejected, oh!

The tulip and the butterfly
appear in coats that are merrier than mine:
if you dress me in the best you can find,
flies, worms and flowers will still outshine me.

ISAAC WATTS, *DIVINE SONGS FOR CHILDREN*

CHOOSE ONE

The two greatest humorists you know are Kafka and Borges. "The Lottery in Babylon" and *The Trial* are sheer joy from beginning to end. Recall Max Brod telling us that when Kafka read him passages from this novel, Kafka almost fell on the floor laughing at what happened to K. Still, the book has a tragic effect on you. It is also appropriate to recall the response to *Don Quixote:* its first readers laughed; the romantics began to weep when they read it, except for the scholars, such as Don Diego Clemencín, who rejoiced if he happened to find a correct sentence in Cervantes; and the moderns don't laugh or cry over the book because they prefer to do their laughing or crying at the movies, and perhaps they are right.

All these idle words, the silly no less than the
Self-regarding and uncharitable, are impediments
in the way of the unitive knowledge of the divine
Ground, a dance of dust and flies obscuring
the inward and the outward Light.

ALDOUS HUXLEY, *THE PERENNIAL PHILOSOPHY*

EVER-PRESENT DANGER

For his own amusement, he writes three pages of false exegesis of one of Góngora's octaves. He piles inanity upon inanity, attributing them to a provincial critic. He types a clean copy. He is certain that everyone who reads it will burst into uncontrollable laughter. He shows his work to four friends who are writers. One understands the joke from beginning to end. Two, enlightened by his example, figure it out a third of the way through, and smile very cautiously. The fourth takes everything with complete seriousness, makes two or three observations just to have something to say, and the author is overcome by embarrassment.

He writes a serious note in which he clarifies once and for all the meaning of the so-called "recalcitrant stanza" by Góngora ("the hedgehog pouch of the chestnut"). He shows it to his four friends. The first denies the validity of his thesis, the other three laugh in amusement, and he is overcome by embarrassment.

I have always hated flies; the tickling sensation
when they land on my brow or bald head—
with the passage of time it amounts to the
same thing; the sound of miniature airplanes
when they buzz around my ears. But what is
truly awful is to see how they land on our
open eyes when we can no longer close them,
how they penetrate the hollows of our nostrils,
how they swarm into an open mouth we
would prefer to keep shut, especially when we
are stretched out, faces to the sun, a rifle
under our shoulder that had been over our
shoulder before, but we had no time to use it.

JOSÉ MARÍA MÉNDEZ

On Sunday I went to the park. In the sun, surrounded by trees, a poet on a bench of indefinite color faced some fifty people who listened to him attentively or casually or courteously.

The poet was reading aloud from papers that he held in his left hand, while with his right he accentuated words when he thought he should. When he finished a poem the applause of his public was so tenuous and unwilling it almost could have been taken for disapproval. The sun shone on all of them with enthusiasm, but all of them had found a way to protect themselves by placing their programs on their heads. A little girl of three and a half pointed out this fact to her father, who also laughed to himself and admired his daughter's intelligence.

The poet, whose clothes were somewhat out of fashion, continued reading. Now he used his body and extended his arms, as if he were sending from his mouth to his public not words but something else, perhaps flowers, or something, although the audience, carefully keeping their balance so that the programs on their heads would not fall, did not respond appropriately to his gesture.

Behind the poet, behind a long table covered with red cloth, sat the judges, looking serious, as they were supposed to. Nearby, on the sidewalk, you could hear the noise of cars passing, sounding their horns; even closer, you really couldn't tell where but in among the trees, a band was playing the William Tell Overture. Both diminished the effect the poet was seeking, but with a certain amount of goodwill it was clear that he was saying something about a spring that dwelled in the heart and a flower that a woman held in her hand that illuminated everything and the conviction that the world in general was fine and only a few small things were needed for the world to be perfect and comprehensible and harmonious and beautiful.

I keep a fly / with golden wings, / I keep a fly / with burning eyes. // It brings death / in its eyes of fire, / it brings death / in its hairs of gold, / its beautiful wings. // I keep it / in a green bottle; / nobody knows / if it drinks, / nobody knows / if it eats. // It wanders the nights / like a star, / it fatally wounds / with its red splendor, / with its eyes of fire. // In its eyes of fire / it carries love, / its blood / gleams in the night, / the love it brings in its heart. // Insect of night, / fly that bears death, / I keep it / in a green bottle, / I love it so well. // But it's true! / It's true! / Nobody knows / if I give it drink, / if I give it food.

ANONYMOUS QUECHUA POEM

TENDER ROSE

It has the advantage of describing the employee closest to you, or yourself, or even the sales manager. "A muddled education, that is, an education full of holes." Once again, as I have for years, I take out my notebook and write down a supposedly ingenious phrase in the hope of using it some day, certain the day will never come, but you can all calm down: This will not be yet another story about the writer who does not write.

Back in the café, a café filled with students and families. The usual matrons come in dressed in their green, yellow, blue blouses, accompanied by their children who are now greedily swallowing ice cream. That pretty lady also asks for pink ice cream for her children Alfonsito, Marito, and Luisito who, when it arrives, methodically smear it on their tongues, their lips, and a little on their hair and cheeks, though Mama gets annoyed and has to tell the oldest that he should learn how to eat because how will Alfonsito ever become a doctor if he doesn't know how to eat and who will set an example for his little brothers if he doesn't.

Outside, it is raining a little. Less. Inside, the panorama of empty tables calms me and makes me think that for a while I won't be bothered as I am when they are occupied and the waiters look at me or it seems to me they're looking at me in fury as if they were telling me to pay up or leave. Another tall, beautiful mother stands and walks decisively to the cashier and moves her hips powerfully and makes me imagine her life and her pretty head, empty but of course happy. I resist the temptation of moving *in mente* to her house and seeing her beside her husband whom she perhaps loves or whom she perhaps deceives or whom perhaps both or whom perhaps neither. The Muzak plays endless arrangements of popular songs that are never interrupted and always seem the same, and meanwhile the doctor comes in and sits down at any table, any table at all, without seeing anyone, distracted or pretending to be distracted. Covering his mouth with his left hand and his left nostril with the first finger of his left hand, as if he were meditating, he says yes when the waiter in the white jacket comes up to him and, as he does every afternoon, asks half seriously, half smiling, if he wants coffee. He has discussed it again with his wife and asked her to understand.

"What is there for me to understand?" she says. "Either you can't or you don't want to, in any case it's all the same." But the fact is that he wants to understand and tries to understand why when he can he doesn't want to and when he wants to he can't, as the vulgar joke says so brazenly about the very young and the very old, except that he is not exceptionally young or exceptionally old but there is something he simply does not understand, why sometimes what seems to be desire changes to repugnance or fear, or why the wise and learned psychiatrist with the fancy tie has to relate everything to his mother as if he were suggesting that he was in love with her (a little old lady!) or depended on her or was dominated by her, but she hasn't lived with him for a long time, she lives far away with a man who isn't his father and she probably never even thinks about him except once in a while at night when she is sad and hates her present husband who pays no attention to her and she tells him how different it all could have been if you had been different while he wipes away the perspiration and cleans, hour after hour, his collection of gold clocks that aren't worth anything because where they live it doesn't matter if time passes or maybe he just doesn't care if it passes and he barely answers with a whisper or a grunt that means she bores him always saying the same thing, so she really is very far away, probably dying right now or dead and maybe right now the telegram is arriving or the maid is nervously answering the telephone and saying she'll give me the message when I come in because I'm not home right now and neither is the Señora. So my mother is my mother, I don't deny it.

"But what can I do?"

"We have to talk. It's a serious problem and we have to discuss it."

"I'm a woman."

"We have to look at our problem."

"Talking doesn't settle anything,"

she says standing, reaching for a cigarette, lighting it, sitting down again, inhaling the smoke, exhaling it blue, looking endlessly at the ceiling while he thinks he has nothing else to say he's already said it so many times and once again he decides to go out to the welcoming, liberating streets. He goes out. It's cold but you still don't need an overcoat, he walks several blocks until he reaches the avenue, eight or ten blocks, it's eleven o'clock and cold even though he doesn't need an overcoat, he walks several blocks and feels tired and takes a bus that goes downtown where he gets off and walks again among the car horns and neon lights and store windows full of shoes, shirts, hats, underwear, shoes, underwear, underwear, shirts, ties, underwear that the woman takes off with indifference in the hotel room revealing her legs, her belly, her sweet breasts that call to him sweetly and touch him while he lies down gently and touches them doing what he has to do with pleasure, thinking about his beautiful pink ice cream while far away someone thinks of him sadly or maybe has just died or is dying right now or while he is smoking someone wants to be with him while he cries with pleasure without being able to explain it to himself while he cries with pleasure without being able to explain anything or wanting to explain anything.

and the animals fornicate directly,
and the bees smell of blood, and the flies
buzz in anger.

PABLO NERUDA, *RESIDENCE ON EARTH*

BREVITY

I frequently hear brevity praised, and I feel a provisional happiness when I hear it said that brevity is the soul of wit.

In Satire 1, I, however, Horace asks himself, or pretends to ask Mecenas, why no one is happy with his condition, why the merchant envies the soldier and the soldier the merchant. You remember, don't you?

The truth is that the writer of short pieces wants nothing more in this world than to write long texts, interminably long texts in which the imagination does not have to work, in which facts, things, animals, and men meet, seek each other out, exist, live together, love, or shed their blood freely without being subjected to the semicolon or the period.

That period, which at this very moment has been imposed upon me by something stronger than myself, something I both respect and despise.

Boy, chase away the flies.

CICERO, *ORATORY*

ERRATA AND FINAL NOTICE

Somewhere on page 45 a comma is missing, omitted consciously or unconsciously by the typesetter who failed to include it on that day, at that time, on that machine; any imbalance this error may cause in the world is his responsibility.

Except for the table of contents, which for unknown reasons comes last in Spanish, the book ends on this page, number 152, which does not mean it could not also begin again here in a backward motion as useless and irrational as the one undertaken by the reader to reach this point.